The Curse of
SANTA CRUZ

Inspired by a True Story

Stephanie Michel

AVIVA
PUBLISHING

New York

AUTHOR'S NOTE AND ACKNOWLEDGMENTS

While living in Santa Cruz, I heard about a curse and decided to investigate. My intention was to do a series of interviews, shoot an independent horror film, and submit it to the festivals for competition. I thought that would take about six weeks. That was back in the year 2000. As I dug deeper and deeper into the history, one thing led to another and more was revealed to me than I ever could have imagined.

I did a series of interviews with the locals, read a number of books, spent countless hours researching at the Museum of Art and History at the McPherson Center, the Santa Cruz Museum of Natural History, and the Santa Cruz Surfing Museum.

First, I would like to thank Richard Hallet for sharing his San Jose State thesis on turn-of-the-last-century entrepreneur and three-time mayor of Santa Cruz, the one and only Fred Swanton, entitled *Never a Dull Moment*. I carried it around with me for two years and read it like a Bible thumper. The detailed information in it was invaluable.

I have a tribe of women in my life who have supported me in the trenches to get through this story. First, I would like to recognize Jill Marie Landis, bestselling author, who took me under her wing and carried me through the painful process of rewrites and character development. She helped me find my Shero. How lucky I am to have met her. I am eternally grateful for my editor, Tyler

Tichelaar, who swooped in and selflessly pasted back the broken pieces of my work here on this heartfelt journey to legitimacy as a writer. I was lost until you held my hand back to the mainstream. I met my best friend, Kim Green, in the fourth grade. Without her unconditional love and support, I never would have pursued any of my dreams. H.F.1 and E.F.2 forever. Love you always. A toast to my friend Carolyn Gerding, my confidant and Rock of Gibraltar. I will always hold you near and dear to my heart. Thank you for your encouragement to move forward and upward in all areas in my life. I could never repay you for all you have done for me. My mother's "black sheep" mentality and fortitude set the tone from the starting gate and gave me the courage to run the race. I have never known a woman with more strength and determination than her. I can only wish that I will continue to follow in her footsteps since she has always been the one who carried me through my darkest hours. I can't forget Elen, my stepmom, whose careful attention to details have proven time after time the importance of thinking things through before you do them. Thank you for my lessons on patience and loving me for who I am. And last, but certainly not least, my dear sister Robin taught me the importance of tolerance and acceptance. It is she who has carried the torch of love and light and given me the gift of compassion.

But the one person I am grateful for most of all is Patrick Orozco of the Parajo Valley Ohlone Indian Council of Watsonville, California. He spent an immense amount of time and energy showing me his ancestors' sacred grounds, their villages, their customs and beliefs, their art, music, and their complete way of life. He also shared the disbelief and dismay of the devastating annihilation of his people. He was my inspiration. Without him, I would not be writing this book.

This novel was first written in a screenplay format and submitted and accepted by a Hollywood production company for development. It attracted a substantial amount of media press. At that time, the story was non-fiction.

For my daughters, Paulina and Pearl.

Thank you for always believing in me. You are the strength that never wavers and keeps me going.

Love, Mom

Let forgiveness be the substitute for fear.
This is the only rule for happy dreams.

— A Course in Miracles

ONE

On August 21, 1961, a blanket of fog covered the entire city of Santa Cruz. The lighthouse horn rang out all night long. Suddenly, loud thumps began to hit buildings throughout the city. Children screamed as dead birds crashed through their windows, landing onto their beds. Parents awoke to the smell of bloody dead birds strewn throughout their homes. Within seconds, the birds covered the beds, tables, floors—any surface where they could land. Outside, birds attacked a man as he screeched and tried to outrun them. The next morning, a band of reporters tried to piece together what had happened the previous night. One local male news reporter lumbered through the bird-strewn streets. His balding head glowed with sweat, and his beady, bloodshot eyes glared into the camera. Spit projected from his thin lips as he reported live on the scene.

"A massive flight of sooty shearwaters, fresh from feasting on anchovies, collided last night with shore-side structures stretching from the City of Santa Cruz to Rio Del Mar."

Not more than five feet away, another female reporter, twenty-two and fresh on the trenches of journalism, tried to compose herself as she quickly looked in a compact mirror.

"Residents were awakened at about 3 a.m. today by a down-pour of birds slamming against their homes, and actually into their homes. Dead and stunted birds littered the streets and roads in the foggy early dawn. Eight people have been injured...."

At the university, Delbert Mann, a museum zoologist, acted as a consultant on a special news broadcast aired throughout the nation.

"The shearwaters generally live in the southern hemisphere. As far as they are concerned, this is their winter flocking area. Often when they are disturbed while feeding, they will rise in flocks above the water. A blinding fog covered the coast last night and this morning. They probably became confused and headed for the only light they could see—streetlights and lamps in peoples' homes. It takes a certain atmospheric condition to cause the confusion of this rare phenomenon."

The broadcast cut to the scenes of Santa Cruz, where bird carcasses, measuring sixteen inches long with a wingspan of three feet, littered the streets, accompanied by dead fish. The entire city smelled like a sardine factory.

"This is disgusting," the female reporter said off-camera as her hand covered her nose.

"What in the hell is going on?"

She tried to shake fish scales off her shoe, but they stuck as if glued to her heel. She walked away from her cameraman.

"I need a drink."

The male reporter standing nearby chuckled.

"It's Armageddon," he said.

"Jesus isn't coming back," she said with a sharp edge.

Then, seemingly out of nowhere, a cloaked Indian woman swiftly passed by her and whispered in her ear.

"It's the curse."

"What did you say?" The reporter turned around, but the woman had already disappeared; no one was standing nearby. She walked over to the male reporter.

"Did you see that person? Who was that? She said it was 'the curse' that did this."

She tried to hold back, but the words just spilled from her mouth.

"Lady, you do need a drink," he said. "There was no one there."

"She was right here. I can't believe you didn't see her. I heard her. I felt her brush up against me. I saw her out of the corner of my eye. She was an American Indian."

"You better make it a stiff one," he mumbled, adding under his breath, "Women reporters. Why don't you go home and be a good wife and a mother like a real woman. This is a man's job."

He stormed off, shaking his head, thinking, "A curse: what next?"

Suddenly, he slipped and fell on fish guts. He tried to get up, but his back seared with pain. Moaning in agony, his voice sounded more like a cow in labor than a man.

"My back. I can't mooove."

Several crewmembers ran over to him, careful not to trip or slide on the carcasses. The female reporter straightened her skirt and jacket, carefully stepped over the fish, and looked down at the man. She could hardly feel sorry for him since he was most definitely the rudest person she had ever met. She shook her head and said, "Tell your troubles to Jesus."

And she walked off.

He popped his head up, screaming, "You blasphemous crazy bitch! You're going to hell!"

His overexertion caused him to screech out with another complaint, only worse this time. "I have a hernia! I think it busted open!"

Very soon after the entire incident in Santa Cruz, Alfred Hitchcock requested a news copy of the reports to research his latest movie project, *The Birds*. He set his story in Bodega Bay, and it featured a series of widespread and violent bird attacks over the course of a few days for unexplained reasons.

Decades later, Rowanna reflected back on days past so long ago. She thought about the obnoxious fat guy who broke his back and then yelled at her. The '60s. Her journalism career.

It was no wonder Alfred Hitchcock worked while residing part-time in Santa Cruz where he spent time with his family and friends. The setting was perfect. "Dark, foggy, beautiful, and mysterious Santa Cruz," she mused.

The curse had returned, after all these years. It was the very reason she began her quest to learn about the real Santa Cruz. Memories flooded her mind: The bird incident. The job in front of the camera and behind the scenes. The Indian woman in the cloak. That whisper, that woman, was the missing link.

Rowanna stood on her deck, shivering in her fuzzy UGGs and her frumpy thirty-year-old light blue slip, which she couldn't imagine living without. She paused and slowly took a long deep breath in through her nose and out of her mouth. She was finally allowing it all to sink in.

She gazed out at the icy, rugged shoreline as her wide, deep blue eyes dripped itchy tears down her prominent cheekbones and off her droopy chin. Her ears felt like they were going to crack right off of her head as her short, wispy gray curls failed to hold in any heat. It had been thirty years. Thirty years of heartache and pain.

It was at this moment when the mental Teflon, which restrained her from knowing who she was as a young woman and had led her to where she was now, cracked as she surrendered to the light of truth that surged in like a flood.

She had endured a long, tough journey, remembering the past and reinventing her life. After the accident, her memories had vanished for what she believed would be forever. Not until this morning could she recount the bird ordeal and that period of her life. Every day, she dedicated herself to trying to recount the course of events that had led up to the night she almost *lost* her life.

Once she came out of the coma, she had to relearn everything she knew. Everything. How to walk, talk, eat, read, and write. The most difficult aspect involved piecing together who she was and where she came from. When she went back to college, she decided to earn her teaching credentials and learned that she had a real knack for history, especially California history.

She could never understand why she knew so many bits and pieces about the place she called home. Now everything began to fall into place.

After she had reported on the bird invasion, she became obsessed with finding out about the curse the Indian woman warned her about. She also became a heavy drinker; addiction counselors might have labeled her as a borderline alcoholic. Her excessive passion to discover the truth led to a course of events that almost put her six feet under. But that was then. And this was now.

She woke up every morning before the sun rose. The minute the clock struck 4:30, she was up and ready. She had given up a long time ago trying to sleep in any later. She shrugged it off as menopause and surrendered to the realization that her day was much more productive when she got a good headstart. She could take her time and enjoy her mornings with the ones she loved most.

Every morning, she would stumble over to her stove and turn on the old black kettle full blast. Once it came to a boil, she would cuddle up on her fluffy purple velvet couch with a cup of herbal tea, as her two black cats snuggled up next to her. Their shiny, lanky legs dangled over the back edges of the couch, making it look like she was wearing them as a fur coat. She gazed into their deep sea-green eyes. The cats were very close to one another and rarely moved from room to room without the presence of the other. Their personalities were more like those of dogs; they had a "pack-like" mentality. She had purchased a $2,000 alkaline-ionizer water machine and hooked it up to her kitchen sink. She said she bought it for herself, but she lied. It was really for her cats, the true loves of her life. She figured with the oxygen and antioxidants it provided, she would save money in vet bills by taking care of the cats in the best way she knew how.

She lived right on the water's edge in a mobile home park. Though she put up with people's beliefs that trailer parks are tacky, she knew this one was different. Anyone would want to live here. It was prime real estate, available by invitation only. She owned the trailer and leased the land. Everyone had tiny, manicured gardens complementing their little yards. It looked like a wonderland, with small, winding roads curving from block to block. Inside, her trailer had hardwood floors and vaulted ceilings and windows throughout, and a large terrace overlooking the oceanic cliffs. Her lot, at the end of West Cliff road, provided the best sunset view in all of Santa Cruz. Nothing compared to the sound of waves crashing, especially when they had a swell. The entire place rumbled and shook, and the smell of the salty mist blended beautifully with her burning "African Seven Peppers Celestial Protection" incense.

She filled her home with large plants, white candles, which she lit every night, and photos of spiritual leaders from throughout the world, including Buddha, Hindu gods, the Dalai Lama, Jesus, Mother Mary, and Paramahansa Yogananda. She also had collected several American Indian relics.

Rowanna O'Connor knew her lifestyle was eccentric, but it suited her because there was nothing ordinary about her. She purposely axed out any chances of having a relationship with another man. She couldn't think of one good reason why anyone would want one in the first place. It wasn't personal against men. She just had no recollection of why she might want a man, and she left it at that.

She came from an Irish/American Indian descent. She didn't want to have to explain over and over again how her drunken father knocked up an Apalachee Indian one night at a casino—that Indian being her mother, of course. The Apalachees originated in northwestern Florida. But their descendants did not live in that location anymore. The tribe was nearly destroyed by war in the early 1700s, and most of the survivors fled to Alabama and Louisiana, where the remaining Apalachee people now lived. Her mother died in a head-on car crash, and her grandmother raised her in the Deep South, in the bayous of southeastern Louisiana.

That was where she either learned or inherited the gift of "sight." Her grandmother taught it to her. Because it came so naturally, her family believed that the gift of intuition is often passed down somehow through the cells in one's genetic makeup.

When she was seventeen, Rowanna packed her bags and left for San Francisco, leaving the swamp behind for good. Her grandmother passed away from natural causes the following spring. She had been raised by two strong women, her mother and grandmother, who taught her well about how to survive. She possessed the skills to do whatever she needed.

She loved the open-minded people of the California coast and the feeling of freedom they gave her. She loved the weather and the creative flow of the area. And best of all, she had been accepted into a university there, with a full scholarship due to her American Indian heritage, to study journalism. It was a place where she could start a brand-new life.

TWO

It was the first day of school at Santa Cruz High. The students scrambled to get to their classes. Every time someone saw an old friend, the two would stop, let out a squeal of delight, and hug after the long summer break.

There were all different types, and they all got along —or so it seemed. There were the surfers, punk rockers, jocks, and nerds. It was just like any other school on the West Coast.

A security guard kept looking suspiciously at everyone from the corner of the long hallway. He was just waiting for something to happen. Anything. His name was Timothy Duffy. He wanted so badly to be the best security guard the school ever had, and with a long history of delinquent misfortunes, he had something to prove, even though he didn't have any family or friends to prove it to. His old friends were all hoodlums, and he was ready for a new and better life. They weren't his real friends anyway. It took him over half of his life to figure that one out.

He grew up on the streets in North Riverdale of the Bronx borough of New York City. It was a thriving Irish community back in the day. But his family struggled, barely surviving. One night when he was eight years old, his father was out drinking with the boys. On his way home, someone stabbed him and left him for dead right above 245th Street. Tim never got over the fact that the police didn't dig deep enough to find any suspects. The case remained unsolved.

The following winter, Tim's mother grew ill and died after a long bout with pneumonia. He ended up in an orphanage, since all of his relatives still lived in Ireland. At age thirteen, he ran away and learned to fend for himself. He never stopped running. His intentions were always good, but the only way he could make enough money was by street fighting. He hoped to become a professional boxer, but he never had the chance. One night, a gang beat him to a pulp in Central Park. They tore his right rotator cuff, leaving him permanently disabled. He resorted to the only thing he knew; he committed petty crimes to survive, traveling from state to state.

When he landed in Santa Cruz, he decided to make a new start. It wasn't as if he had an epiphany or felt at home; he simply had run as far as he could. There was nowhere left to hide, and he grew weary of rambling from place to place. He decided to play it straight, to see whether he could scrape together enough integrity and courage to contribute to society, rather than detract from it. It had been coming for some time: that little voice in his head and the aching in his heart, which yearned for some sort of life purpose.

Living in Santa Cruz made him feel like he did before his parents died—like he had potential to be anyone he wanted to be. He began walking with more ease, breathing a little deeper. He remembered what safety felt like, what it felt like before he became an orphan. As he returned to the same bed each night, everything about Santa Cruz began to seem right.

A job as a security guard seemed like the perfect fit; after all, he knew all about petty-criminal minds. Ironically, just about anyone could get a job as a security guard in Santa Cruz. And he excelled at his job; he could spot punk thieves by the way they looked at him—just enough to size him up but not long enough to make eye contact. No one could get past him, and nothing surprised him. He tended to watch the evening news with his uniform on. Every time he heard about the latest crime, he'd finger his badge as his past burglaries flashed through his mind. He finally had a chance to set the record straight once and for all—to be the man he knew he could.

Rowanna pushed her way through the crowd, her hands full of books and loose papers. The striking sixty-year-old caused people to do a double take. Though she didn't bother to tweeze the dark hairs on her chin, she dressed up every day in a jacket suit and long skirt covering the thick beige stockings she wore in an attempt to hide her varicose veins.

She didn't fit in with the other teachers at Santa Cruz High, usually older hippies with graying long hair who, after around their mid-thirties, decided to take a "real job," mainly for medical insurance. A handful of teachers were dedicated to academia; they published books and taught out of their altruistic need to give back to the community. The one thing the artistic hippies had in common with the intellects was their love for the earth. They implemented recycling programs within the high school before "going green" became a catch phrase. Most composted and grew organic gardens in their backyards. They tended to consider themselves vegetarians, even though they ate chicken and fish.

Tim couldn't help but lose his train of thought whenever Rowanna walked past him. Though Tim tried to keep his eyes on the lockers and the teenagers holding hands and digging in their pockets, Rowanna always caught his eye for more than a fleeting moment.

She knew she caused disturbances. She had heard kids, and even teachers, whisper as she squeezed through the mass of bodies to reach her room.

"I heard she was a witch," was the first comment.

The second one was: "I hope to God that's not my teacher."

She had to walk by the football players' lockers on the way to her classroom. The wide receiver, Eric Swanson, caught her eye. At sixteen, he had already established a reputation with the girls as frisky and "born for action." He puckered his lips and blew Rowanna a kiss. Everyone laughed. She rolled her eyes and grabbed the door handle. She couldn't open it fast enough.

"You are one sick dude, you know that," Eric's teammate Thomas said. Thomas was an African American whose intelligence balanced his brawn.

Eric's best friend, "bad boy" Randy Lopez, pulled out his schedule of classes.

"Dude! We both have her!"

The other guys standing around looked at their schedules. "You poor bastards!" Thomas said. He playfully shoved Eric, pleased he didn't have the withered teacher.

"Don't worry; you'll have her next semester," Eric shouted.

"Yeah! When we're done with her!" Randy said. He was on a roll. "I'm gonna get her from the front, and Eric, you can take her from behind."

"Gross!" Thomas said, rubbing his hand across his chin. "She has a beard!"

The boys all laughed and smacked each other hard on the backs. Then Eric paused. There was a girl standing next to them. Her name was Holly Hartford. She was a tall and leggy blonde cheerleader. Eric had flirted with her before, but she didn't want anything to do with him.

"That'll take about thirty seconds. Don't flatter yourself." She slammed her locker closed and walked away.

Randy yelled after her, "Oh yeah? Well, you've never had a Latino lover baby; that's your problem!"

Holly walked right into the arms of Conrad "Viper" Washborn, otherwise known as "Prince Charming"—only a sickening incarnation of the fairytale lover. He escorted her to their first class in room nine, Ms. Rowanna O'Connor's class.

Tim now had his first big conflict of the school year. He walked up to the boys in the hall slowly, while he patted the top of his baton, which dangled off of his belt buckle. He crackled his gum as he chewed it, which made him seem even more like a washed-up, underpaid has been. Worst of all, he wore a toupee to cover his bald spot. He felt there was no greater shame than for a "tough guy" like him to grow bald. He would rather die a thousand slow and painful deaths than lose the hair on his head. He knew the wig didn't look natural, but better the synthetic wig than the shiny, pasty, eye-magnet on the very top of his head. His voice sounded like Clint Eastwood in *Dirty Harry*, with a sort of a growl, as if he had swallowed a cup of gravel for breakfast.

"You boys better be moving on to your classes now, or you'll be cleaning up the school at lunch—in front of everybody, in your gym shorts."

The boys looked at each other and tried not to laugh. "Whatever, dude," Eric mumbled under his breath, as he turned away from Tim.

Randy took a different approach. He got right up in Tim's face, saying, "Ooohhh we're scared—Freak!" Then he quickly turned and walked to class.

Tim didn't know what to say. He just assumed the kids would respect authority. He stood there, with his baton in his hand, trying to come up with Plan B. Yes, he now had an idea of who some of the kids were and what he was going to be dealing with. He wrote down their physical descriptions and placed his notebook back in his pocket.

THREE

The students piled into the classroom. Howard Chin and Giliano Lombardi had already taken the front row seats. They were best friends, and they were nerds.

Eric stared down Giliano, who had vowed not to give in this time. But Eric didn't budge. "What?" Giliano asked.

"I'm just trying to see what your face is going to look like with your lips all puckered up around your gums after I knock all of your teeth out," Eric replied.

An ugly visual raced through Giliano's mind. Was it really worth taking the chance of losing his teeth? "He's just trying to scare me. How could he get away with it anyway?" he thought to himself.

Still, Giliano didn't want to take any chances. He got up and moved to the next closest seat to the front. He was never a backseat guy. The scumbags sat in the back, which always left plenty of seats in the middle of the room. He hated sitting behind people, though. He could see and hear better in the front row.

"You suck, Eric," he stated as bravely as he could as Eric slid into his former seat.

Howard, on the other hand, refused to get up from his seat. Randy entered the room and started spouting out racist names to get him to move, but the teacher interrupted him. Randy walked to another seat, swiping his hip into Howard's shoulder and whispering, "I'll get you later."

"Hello, everyone; my name is Ms. Rowanna." Rowanna pointed to the board, where she wrote her name. "In case anyone didn't hear me, that is 'Ms.' Please don't forget it."

"What's the difference between Miss, Mrs., and Ms.?" Eric shouted out.

She ignored him.

"I'm going to go over my class rules and tell you about some of the material we will be covering. Then, if we still have time, we can get to know each other a little bit.

"So let's begin: The first rule is simple. It's something you learned back in kindergarten."

She looked at Eric. "And that is, if you have a question, please raise your hand. Rule number two: Be respectful."

Right about then, Viper, seated in the back, disbursed a spit wad through a straw at Giliano. It hit him hard and landed on the back of his neatly shaven neck with a splash. Giliano grunted as he pulled out a Kleenex from his coat pocket and wiped it off manically. He had a germ phobia. If there was anything worse to him than other people's bodily smells, it was their germ-infested saliva. He panicked, incessantly wondering whether the torture would ever end.

Rowanna looked over at Viper and continued. "I won't tolerate any monkey business."

Randy ignored her speech, obsessing about how Howard would pay for refusing to change seats. His attention-deficit disorder came in handy when he wanted to plot revenge, but it was the only time he could actually focus on one thing for any amount of time.

Rowanna continued:

"Santa Cruz is very rich in history. We won't have nearly enough time to get through all of it. Oh, and in case you're not sure where you are," she pointed to the writing on the board, "this class is: The History of Santa Cruz."

FOUR

As the waves crashed on the rocks, they sounded like a jet taking off. Santa Cruz was known for its beauty: pristine coastal beaches and sharp, rocky cliffs with hot-pink and fire-red flowers spilling over the sides. Most days, seals and sea otters playfully slipped in and out of the emerald green water.

But danger lurked there, too. Next to a century-old lighthouse stood a sign that read: "Don't be next! Since 1965, 92 people have drowned along our coastal cliffs and beaches. Many of these deaths were preventable. Help prevent accidents. Stay behind the fences. Stay away from the cliffs' edges. Respect the ocean!"

A group of guys stood on a cliff, watching surfers wait for another set to roll in. One surfer took off on a huge wave. Another surfer took off on the same wave and came up behind the first, punching him in the side of the head and shoving him off of his board.

"Fucking Tranny! Go home!" the surfer yelled.

The guys on the cliff laughed. From their vantage point, they could see how one beach led to another. They stood adjacent to dog beach, where dogs ran wild with their owners. There weren't many places left where you could legally walk dogs on the beach. The residents of Santa Cruz had fought hard for the dog beach.

Other beaches catered to various special demographics. The nudist beach wasn't far from dog beach. Teenagers often snuck down to the beach to fawn over well-endowed bodies—and make fun of the not-so-well-endowed. Most of the women at the nudist beach didn't shave. The kids used to joke about how a person could get lost in the jungle of their unruly glory. They considered them perfect candidates for a centerfold in *National Geographic*. But the actual beach-goers didn't seem to care. They ignored any onlookers and simply enjoyed nature.

Past all of these beaches sat the boardwalk. Most Santa Cruz residents spent a considerable amount of time on the boardwalk at the lively municipal pier, the amusement park, and the bowling alley. At any given time of the day, people of all ages filled the area.

One particular day, an African American man was fishing off the rocks, drinking cheap beer. He loved cheap beer. The lightness of the barley flavor, the crispy, cold, bubbly that ran down his thirsty throat, and the price made him love the brew. It reminded him of good times, times when he was free to do anything and be anything, with no attachments. As he sat drinking, he thought about how he loved this environment: the smell of the salty air that streamed up his nostrils and the mist of the waves as they crashed upon the rocks. This was going to be one of the best days he'd ever had; he could feel it. He held his rod, waiting for a big one to bite, but he really didn't care whether he caught one or not.

He had brought his family to Santa Cruz to start a new life. He had an adoring wife, and his son, who filled him with pride, attended Santa Cruz High School. The boy had made the honor roll and was college bound with a full scholarship to boot. Life was at its finest, and nothing could break his mood that day. He was about as grateful as grateful gets.

He looked up to see a group of birds flying overhead. The sun's glare blinded him for a moment, but he knew the circling birds signaled fish.

Suddenly, a large, rogue wave came in and sucked him up. It wasn't any louder than any of the other waves, and it came out of nowhere. He had no warning at all. As he slipped into the dark-green, watery vacuum, he couldn't even process what had happened. Silence and warmth engulfed his entire being. The tug-of-war between his worldly relationships and the one he had with his Maker pulled him from left to right, up and down, and everywhere around. He couldn't swim, and as he choked on water, he struggled to remain conscious. When his head hit a jagged rock with the undertow, it felt as if it had cracked wide open: He saw his whole life spill out like a movie on fast-forward, from the time he was born until now. He felt as if he had a choice to leave or stay.

He knew automatically.

His head was too severely injured. It was game-over. Within seconds, he was gone forever.

It all happened so quickly; no one ever saw a thing.

FIVE

Rowanna was familiarizing the class with the required literature and curriculum.

"I don't use a regular textbook in my class. But there is some required reading, and we will host two guest speakers, as well. I want everyone to read *The Ohlone Way* by Malcolm Margolin and *Santa Cruz Is in the Heart* by Geoffrey Dunn."

She held up copies of the books in each hand.

"If you can't get them in the library, buy them at Book Shop Santa Cruz. We will also be reading portions of *Chinese Gold* by Sandy Lydon."

She held up the book.

"You will need these books with you at all times while you are in my class. If you have any problems obtaining them, please come see me, and we will work something out."

She slowly climbed out of her chair and walked around the room, looking at each student. She stopped at Eric's desk and tapped her wrinkled finger on his desk.

"You should be writing this down."

He opened his backpack and pulled out a notebook and a pen. The rest of the students followed his lead.

"It breaks the flow of my lectures to repeat myself, so I expect everyone to have a pad and something to write with on their desks for the entire semester. If you miss out on something, I expect you to get the information from a fellow classmate after class. You need to stay alert at all times. Let there be no mistake. *You will be tested.*"

The students were scared. What was that supposed to mean? Her foreboding tone made it sound like the test wouldn't just be oral or written. They would be tested in *other ways*.

"In what 'other' ways?" most of them wondered.

"Creepy!" That's what Holly thought. "She's so creepy—with the outfit and the weird voice, too. I've already had enough of this crazy lady."

Leslie Lopez was a beautiful Latin-American Indian girl who sat in the back. Normally, only the scumbags and druggies sat in the back, but she didn't know that: She was new and shy. Rowanna glared at her, sizing her up. Leslie was the only one in class, other than Howard and Giliano, who pulled out a pad and pen before the teacher made the announcement.

"I want you to read at least two chapters every night if you expect to keep up in my class. You can start with *The Ohlone Way*. It will give you some insight into the history of the people who first lived here. You should be finished with it by the end of next week when we will discuss it."

She looked at the Indian girl again.

"What is your name?"

Eric turned around to see the girl sitting way in the back. He had to do a double take because he couldn't believe his eyes. He hadn't noticed her when he first came in the room. She must have gotten there before him. She had long, black hair. She was wearing a white V-neck shirt. The tight blue jeans cut off some of the circulation around her hips, but no one would have guessed because she was so skinny. She wore large, natural feathered earrings, a turquoise heart necklace, and a matching sterling silver ring. It was as if a golden aura surrounded her: He fell instantly in love. He thought he heard birds singing. Were there really birds chirping outside the window, or was he imagining things? Randy noticed the look on Eric's face before he turned to look for himself. Then he whipped his head around to get a second glance.

"Wow. Where did she come from?" Randy thought to himself.

Two jealous born-again surfer girls, Bliss and Jade, looked at her too. Then they gave each other "the look," straightened their posture, and simultaneously waved at Randy. He mischievously waved back.

The new girl spoke up.

"My name is Leslie."

"Leslie what?" asked the teacher.

"Leslie Lopez."

"Hey, that's my last name too!" Randy interrupted.

The class giggled.

"Is that so?" Rowanna said. "Maybe you two are related."

"I hope not!" Randy blurted out.

Rowanna looked at him inquisitively.

"And why is that?"

"Oh, I ahhh…" Randy stumbled on his words.

The class laughed.

"So you two have never met?"

"I just moved here in July, from Watsonville," said Leslie.

"Well, welcome, Leslie. Maybe someone from class can show you around," the teacher said.

Eric raised his hand eagerly.

"I can show her around," he blurted out.

"What is your name?"

"Eric, ma'am. Miss, I mean, uh, Ms. Rowanna."

Everyone laughed.

"Welcome to you, too, Eric," she replied. "I can tell you're going to be a lot of fun to have in my class. I hope you keep your seat up here in front. I wouldn't want you to miss out on anything."

Holly heard it again in Ms. Rowanna's tone—something creepy. What was it with this teacher and her wicked, weird voice and irritating secret code words? "Give me a break!" she thought.

But Eric didn't seem to notice. He was in another world. With Leslie in attendance, nothing could go wrong. It was almost too much to take. He knew he was going to love this class.

Rowanna continued.

"Instead of taking roll, I would like everyone to write their name on this sheet of paper I am passing around. I would prefer you to keep the seating arrangement the way it is. Please keep in mind that I have five other classes, and this system makes it easier for me to get to know everyone."

She handed the paper to Eric first.

Howard turned around to Randy. Randy stared back at him, and Howard could read his lips: "I am going to get you."

"Who knows anything about our local history?" Ms. Rowanna asked.

Nobody responded. She figured they were just a little uncomfortable—it being their first period on the first day back to school.

"Are you all being shy?"

Still no response. Jade swung her leg back and forth. She cleared her throat and raised her hand. Ms. Rowanna happily nodded to her.

"We learned about the Ohlone Indians in the fourth grade, but I don't really remember anything other than making clay missions. We used to smoke a lot of pot back then."

The class laughed as Bliss nodded her head in agreement. As she raised her hand to speak, her purple spaghetti strap camisole revealed that she didn't shave, just like Jade. Randy gasped aloud at her hairy armpits. He looked over at Eric, and they laughed. Bliss ignored them, speaking softly.

"The Christians came and taught the Indians how to live." Ms. Rowanna interrupted her.

"They were actually Spanish Catholic priests. Did the Indians not know how to live before Christ?"

"Absolutely not!" Bliss said, raising her voice.

Jade waved her hand high in the air this time. The hairs stood straight up and out from under her arms. Randy shrieked again.

"Oh, my God!"

Ms. Rowanna shot him a stern look and asked the young lady what her name was.

"Jade. My name is Jade."

Both Jade and Bliss wore revealing, psychedelic clothing that looked like it had been bought from a 1970s thrift shop. They both had long, curly, dirty blonde hair and were fair-skinned, with freckles. They were not sisters—they weren't even related—but everyone mistook them for twins.

"It's not that the Indians didn't know how to live. It's just that it's such a miracle that the Lord found them so that when they died, their souls could go to heaven," Jade said. "Think of all of those years they lived with no spirituality, whatsoever. I mean, it's so sad."

Holly rolled her eyes. Viper laughed aloud. The class began joking.

"Here we go again," Rowanna thought to herself.

"So, so sad," Bliss added to Jade's comment.

"Anyone else?" Ms. Rowanna asked.

Leslie raised her hand.

"The Indians never took more than they needed. They were around way before Christ was born. They sang with the birds. They swam with the whales, and they danced with the wind. How could anyone think they weren't spiritual?"

Now things were cooking. Ms. Rowanna was pleased with the diverse belief system she had here. It was going to make a stimulating, well-rounded group for her planned debates.

"How do you know all of this, Leslie?"

"My grandmother taught me."

Ms. Rowanna raised her eyebrows in approval.

"Does anyone know anything about the Chinese or how tourism came to town?"

"Eric's great-grandfather built the casino and the boardwalk," Randy blurted out.

The teacher wanted to encourage discussion, but it was more important for her to establish some order and control first.

"Could we please raise our hands first before we speak?" she said.

Howard looked back at Randy. Randy gave him the evil eye again. Howard slid down in his seat, wondering what Randy was going to do to him later. Ms. Rowanna turned her attention to Eric.

"Is this true, Eric?"

"Yes, ma'am! I mean, Rowanna."

The class laughed.

"I mean, Ms. Rowanna."

When the last person signed the attendance sheet and handed it to Ms. Rowanna, she searched for Eric's last name. She raised her eyebrows.

"Your last name is Swanson?"

He nodded.

"That's quite a name. Are you aware of your family history?"

"Like the back of my hand," Eric said.

"I heard there is a curse," someone in the back of the room murmured. Rowanna was shocked.

"Who said that?"

Holly pointed to her boyfriend, Viper.

"Did you say that?" Ms. Rowanna asked Viper.

"Yeah, ma'am. If you're not married by the time you're thirty, you're cursed to wander the streets aimlessly, forever. That's why we have so many bums. And whoever moves here can never get away, not for long that is. They always come back—always. Everyone knows about the curse."

Rowanna straightened her thick navy skirt.

"Interesting. This is going to be a very exciting class. My, how time flies when you are having fun," she said, just seconds before the bell rang.

Randy rushed for the door. Jade whispered, "She wasn't even looking at the clock."

"Yeah, how did she know the bell was going to ring?" Bliss asked.

Both girls had large crosses hanging from their necks. Jade fingered hers, saying, "Praise the Lord!"

"Amen, sister. Amen," Bliss agreed.

Rowanna yelled over the students piling out of the room. "I have a special guest coming in tomorrow—don't be late. And whoever is wearing the patchouli oil, don't put it on before you come into my class. The smell makes me queasy. Showers are much more practical."

Jade and Bliss smelled each other and then their wrists, glancing at the teacher. "Whatever," they said, simultaneously.

SIX

Howard and Giliano stood in the restroom, talking over the sinks. Giliano tried to scrub the germs off the back of his neck, and then he turned his attention to his hands, soaping all the way up his arms, in a vain attempt to clear his memory of the spit wad Viper blew on him in class.

"Ms. Rowanna is the weirdest teacher I have ever had. How am I going to stay focused on my studies?"

"Don't you see?" Giliano said with excitement. "Her weirdness is exactly what's going to keep us focused. This is the easiest 'A' we'll ever get!"

Suddenly, they heard someone moan in one of the stalls. "Help me, please…"

It sounded like a little girl's voice.

"What was that?" Howard asked in a shaky voice.

"Is there a little girl in there?" Giliano asked, not believing the high-pitched voice could belong to a boy.

Howard cautiously walked toward the stall; as soon as he opened the door and peeked in, a powerful force sucked him in. Giliano panicked and ran to help, as he watched Howard's body move out of control. The stall door slammed and hit Giliano in the face. He was knocked out cold. All Howard could hear was Indian drumming.

"Where did that come from? Why can't I see anything?" he asked, rubbing his sore head.

It all happened so fast; he didn't know what had hit him. Then he saw Randy's face. Randy spoke just like a little girl. It was surreal.

"Don't you ever, ever, ever disrespect me again because I will fucking kill you."

His voice faded in and out from boy to girl to man.

"I will beat you to a pulp."

Randy pumped Howard's head in and out of the toilet water and left him there.

"Mother-fucking geeks."

He kicked Giliano in the ribs just for good measure on his way out. Howard came to and crawled out from the stall, dripping wet and coughing. Once he caught his breath, he collapsed on Giliano, who was bleeding. When Randy slammed the door in Giliano's face, it broke his nose. Howard began to cry.

"I am sorry. I am so sorry, my friend."

SEVEN

Rowanna stood on her mobile home terrace at the end of the day, wearing her white terrycloth robe and drinking a cup of peppermint tea. The cats rubbed up against the varicose veins protruding from her calves.

As the sun set, the sky transformed into vibrant shades of dark purple and orange. She ran through all of the classes and the children she remembered in her mind. Only first period stuck out. In this particular class, these children—these young adults, she reminded herself—were tuned into a different frequency and didn't even know it. She believed any given person was six degrees of separation from knowing everyone else on the planet. And here they all sat in one class; it seemed nearly incestuous to her. Little did they know how close they were to the past and how it could—and most definitely would—affect their future. Didn't they know that in one single moment, their whole way of life could change? Everything as they knew it, gone—wiped clean.

She recalled how invincible she thought she was when she was a teenager. The world was her oyster. She was smart and beautiful. Her grandmother used to tell her, "There are two kinds of people in this world: will nots and cannots. Are you a will not or are you a cannot?"

Rowanna felt sure that this year would be the time to tie all of the loose strings together that led her to become the person she had. Most people would never view her as insecure.

But most people didn't know what she had gone through.

She knew that deep down she was a bit of a recluse and that it wasn't good for her to live like that. But then again, she interacted with plenty of people when school was in session, and that was enough stimulation for her.

She slowly bent down and spoke softly to her beloved cats as she stroked them. "Besides, you are plenty enough for this old woman," she chuckled. "Plenty."

EIGHT

The following morning, an electrical storm brewed. The clouds swirled outside the classroom windows.

An Indian man in his fifties sat quietly in the front of the classroom as the students shuffled in and took their seats. His jet-black hair was tied in a ponytail, and he wore everyday street clothing. But he had headgear on and wore a bear-claw necklace.

Ms. Rowanna introduced him. "Today, we have a guest speaker, and his name is Dennis."

Holly rolled her eyes and sunk down in her chair. "What could be more boring than this?" she thought to herself. "He doesn't even have an Indian name. What a crock." She whispered to Viper, "Wake me up when it's over."

Ms. Rowanna continued: "He is a descendant and Shaman Elder of the Ohlone Indian Nation."

Just as Holly started drifting off into her morning nap, Dennis stood and shook some instruments he pulled from his pocket. He walked around the room, looking every student in the eye, as he dropped the instruments on various desks. Then he stopped at Randy's desk and let out a bloodcurdling scream. Lightning lit up the sky as the lights in the room flickered. Holly screamed too.

"Jesus, Holly!" Viper said, with an edge to his voice. "Make up your mind. Go to sleep or stay awake, but don't do that again. You're freaking me out."

"He's freaking me out!" she exclaimed.

Dennis dropped his head down, and the students heard thunder outside. When he dramatically popped his head back up, Randy saw a bear face, with red eyes, in place of Dennis' face. No one else noticed. For some reason only Randy could see it.

"Is it the demons in me that are connecting with the demons in Dennis?" Randy wondered. The angry part of him welcomed as much evil as he could invite. But another part of him shook with fear.

Only Randy's dark side could feed his insatiable hunger for the empty void that consumed his broken heart. Consciously, he knew this, but unconsciously, he just felt like a confused and angry young man—the ultimate victim. He blamed everyone else for his pain, and violence was his only way out. Somehow, Dennis knew this. He saw Randy's bleeding heart and despair. He just wanted to shake Randy up a little—get his attention. What Randy didn't know was that there was more in store for him. Much more.

Dennis propped himself up on a shelf by an open window.

"A long time ago, there lived a powerful nation of people called the Ohlone Indians. It was a time when wildlife thrived in Santa Cruz. Most people living here today would have to see it to believe it. The skies held millions of birds—thousands of different species."

Outside the classroom, the dark skies brightened and filled with flocks of birds. It was as if his story dictated the weather.

He had Holly's full attention now. She nudged Viper and whispered to him.

"Look outside. How can that be?" she asked, dumbfounded. Dennis ignored the whispers.

"My ancestors told me there were so many birds that when they flew in front of the sun, it was like a solar eclipse. It happened on a regular basis."

The birds flew against the backdrop of the sun, and the sky went from dark to sunny again. Now he had everyone's full attention.

"Deep in a redwood forest, an eagle perched proudly on top of a three-hundred-year-old tree before he took flight. His heavy wings labored through the ancient dark canopies. He soared high above the mountains. Trees and blue sky stretched as far as the naked eye could see.

"Sixteen thousand years ago, freshwater lakes covered Scotts Valley, providing plenty of food for my people and the local inhabitants, which in those days included mammoths and saber-toothed tigers.

"The huge San Lorenzo River ran right through the City of Santa Cruz. The fish were so abundant that it looked like they were swimming backwards. Only those with open minds and open hearts can see it now," he paused. "Open to what, you might ask yourself? Think big. Very big. Like Adam and Eve in the beginning. Now think even bigger. Consider living in perfect balance with nature and each other. Think about compassion, courage, and commitment."

He looked over at Randy sadly.

"Imagine forgiveness, real forgiveness."

Randy knew exactly what Dennis was talking about. But how did Dennis know anything about him?

Bliss raised her hand in a trance-like state.

"I don't understand. How can you refer to the Bible and use Jesus' name in vain?"

Jade raised her hand next, but she didn't wait to be called upon.

"Exactly. There was no perfect harmony for people or nature until Jesus died for our sins."

"Oh, my God, you've got to be kidding me," Viper yelled out and started to laugh.

The rest of the class laughed nervously, except for Leslie.

The clouds rolled in again and lightning struck. It lit up the whole sky, eliciting screams from the students.

"I need you to hold your questions until Dennis is finished," Ms. Rowanna said to the girls. "And Viper, keep quiet."

Viper shook his head in disgust. Just then, thunder rattled the entire room. The storm had settled over the school. Dennis was just beginning.

"Now, let's take a look back in time. Let's say three hundred years ago or so…"

The students found themselves slipping back into a place and time that seemed to be real, only it was so long ago that it seemed as if they were trapped in a time capsule entering another dimension. Dennis began to tell the story of the Ohlone Indians.

NINE

"One day, long before the white man arrived, three young men came home from a fishing trip. Two of them carried huge salmons, steelheads and sturgeons over their shoulders, while the third filled his outstretched arms with wood, harpoons, fishing poles, and a net. The elders, who were sitting under a tule shade, saw the young men and began to clap and cheer, nudging each other as if they had placed bets on the outcome of dinner. Children ran to greet the young men, hoping to hear their stories of adventure. A beautiful girl peeked out from behind a tree to catch the first glimpse of her love after a long day without him. His catch would surely please her father. It was just another day in paradise.

"It wasn't until the white man arrived on the shores of Santa Cruz that the civilization of my people began to crumble."

No one saw—not even Holly—but just then Viper's eyes grew dark red with rage, and his lips buckled tight around the sides as he glared at Dennis with a vengeance. Dennis looked back at him with acknowledgment. He knew who he was. Viper let out a gut-wrenching scream. It sounded like a wounded dinosaur—maybe a tyrannosaurus rex—caving in from its own weight. The sound vibrated from deep within Viper. The class screamed. Bliss and Jade held hands and prayed quietly. Holly grabbed hold of Viper, and suddenly, his symptoms vanished.

"Viper—look at me. I'm scared," she said, trembling.

Viper gave her a dazed look, and then he slumped into his chair, embarrassed. Dennis continued as if nothing had happened. He knew the day had finally arrived for the truth to be brought into the light.

"Once upon a time, there was an English ship that got caught in a winter storm and crashed into the rocky shores of Santa Cruz. It was a cold and thick foggy night. But the moon was full. Through the thunderous clouds and fog, a blue moonlight haze lightened the sky.

"The ship's captain barked orders at his crew in hopes of salvaging their lives. But the men couldn't bail the water out faster than it poured in, and the ship began to sink. They couldn't fight the twenty-foot waves as the ship pounded into razor-sharp rocks. One by one, they fell overboard or slipped through the cracks of the broken vessel and were left for dead.

"But legend has it that, the following morning, a local tribesman found a lone survivor of the shipwreck off the coast of West Cliff. The sun shone on this white man's leathery face as his body lay washed up on a rock. He had long gray hair and a beard. His lips curved inward, snug around his toothless gums. The tribesman leaned over the cliff to get a good look at the Englishman. The tribesman felt afraid but also curious. He cautiously moved closer and closer, and then returned to his tribe to tell them about the man.

"The tribelet took the white man in and nursed him back to health. Within days, the old man sat up in the tule hut as my ancestors circled and stared at him. As pale as he was, they thought he might have some sort of sickness—or worse, be under a bad spell, the possible works of a Shaman or an evil spirit. Though they remained weary of him, they continued to provide him with the necessities to survive and the genuine hospitality my people have always been notorious for.

"One morning, a young maiden served him warm tea. He looked at her with lustful eyes, but she was too young to realize it. But the others noticed. The next day, accompanied by two others, she brought the Englishman food. His provocative stares upset her companions, and they reported his behavior to the chief, who became enraged with the man's disrespect, especially after they had saved his life.

"'Now he thinks he is going to run off with one of our precious young maidens!'

"The chief sentenced the Englishman to death immediately.

"On the night of the Englishman's proclaimed death, as they tied him to a tree, one of the tribesmen begged the chief not to kill the Englishman; he claimed it would bring bad luck to the tribe. The chief ignored the tribesman. So later that night, the tribesman set the Englishman free and led him to safety. When the chief found out, he sentenced the Indian to death, in place of the white man.

"As the young tribesman drowned in the San Lorenzo River by the hands of his very own people, he cursed his tribe and the land they lived upon, promising to haunt Santa Cruz forever. Old Chepa, an elderly Branciforte woman, calls this river ghost Pogonip, meaning 'Icy Fog.'"

Loud thunder and lightning struck outside the classroom again. All of the girls huddled together in the center of the room. Viper slid out of his seat and exited through the back door.

"Where are you going?" Holly yelled out to him. She was terrified and didn't want to be left alone.

He never looked back to answer.

Water started seeping in through open windows. Ms. Rowanna began closing them, and when Eric got up to help her, all of the windows slammed shut on their own.

Dennis sat patiently and waited until Ms. Rowanna settled the students back into their seats. Then he continued:

"Not long afterward, a fierce group of Yachicume Indians from Stockton invaded Santa Cruz, slaughtering the locals. Some escaped, and then they returned several years later to perform a ceremony on Mission Hill. They asked for peace, forgiveness, and guidance from the three great spirits: Coyote, Eagle, and Hummingbird.

"As the ceremony came to a crescendo, a sudden earthquake occurred, causing the Yachicumes to run for shelter in the hills. Santa Cruz was once again home for the Ohlones, only they were to face more despair than one could ever imagine. This is our love, this is our fear, and this is our story."

Suddenly, as if nothing had ever happened, the weather cleared, and the students appeared more at ease.

TEN

Dennis continued with the story of the Ohlone Indians.

"Flying fast over the cliffs, a seagull landed on the sands of Natural Bridges Beach. It was a warm and sunny day. About a half-acre up from the shore, a sub-tribelet had set up camp. The rest of the tribelet was about a mile away. The length of their stays on the beach depended upon the weather—it might be a day or a week, or even longer.

"They rejoiced: Two of the men were teaching three boys how to fish from the rocks. The tallest one was wearing a shark tooth necklace, which his grandfather gave him. He rubbed one of the teeth between two fingers and remembered the story his grandfather had told him.

"When his grandfather was a young man, he went spear fishing in the great sea. Everything went well, until he felt a great bump on the tule boat. Then he felt another one—then another, even stronger. At first, he thought it was a whale. But as fate would have it, it turned out to be a great white shark. He began to fight for his life. With the fourth thud, the shark came directly out of the water with his mouth wide open.

"Remember the movie *Jaws*? The sharks were related," Dennis said, as he let out a chuckle. No one else laughed.

"As the shark showed his teeth," Dennis continued, "the young man thrust his entire spear down into the beast's throat, killing him instantly. When he dragged it back to shore, working patiently with the tides for one entire day and night, he became the most famous fisherman of all time.

"Moments later, the boy was back in the heat of the moment when he thought he had caught a big one. He wrestled with his spear, screaming with excitement, when suddenly an elder jumped out of the water, laughing hysterically, waving the spear triumphantly high into the air. Five other elders watched under the tule shade, eating various nuts and berries. They, too, could hardly contain themselves.

"The boy, utterly embarrassed, quickly walked away to his campsite. There, he spotted a beautiful young woman, one he had known his whole life. He noticed a strange look in her eye, unlike anything he had seen before. Although they were the same age, she was much taller, and more mature. She had body hair and small, round breasts. She gazed at him with eyes of desire. He felt stunned, as if she could see through his flesh, to his very soul. His fear caused him to run to seek comfort in his mother, who was breast-feeding her new baby. He looked adoringly at his new little sister. His mother stroked the top of his head as he rubbed his baby sister's cheeks.

"'How quickly they grow big,' his mother thought to herself as she twisted her son's long, black hair around her finger. 'He will be gone soon to sleep with another,' she thought, sadly.

"She remembered his birth as if it were yesterday, and oh, what a beautiful day it was. She would have been happy to do it all over again if she could. He looked exactly like his father, and she was sure her son would choose the mate the great spirits intended for him.

"From a nearby hilltop, the boy's father watched his family. He was tall and handsome, like his son, with high cheekbones and deep brown eyes. Only his eyes curled upward in the corners, as if invisible strings pulled them up. Yes, he looked different from the rest, causing some to wonder silently about what had happened a long time ago, before he was born, when his own mother got lost in the woods. But no one dared say a word about it; they treated him as just as much a part of the family as everyone else.

"As he kept an eye on his family, the father worked on his bow. He was the most highly respected hunter in the tribe, not only because of his natural-born talent, but also because of his generosity. He gave everything he had to offer with great love and dignity. Though the new bow he worked on was his most prized possession, he could not help gaze at his beautiful family. He was so proud. His wife caught him staring and blew him a kiss. He stretched his hand upward as far as he could and caught the kiss as if she missed the mark. She laughed. He kept the kiss clenched in his fist and lightly tapped his chest three times. A group of women giggled at the sight as they crushed acorns for dinner.

"The heaviest woman of the group looked over to her husband. He was the one who tricked the boy in the water with the spear. The man was the Shaman of the tribe. They said he had eyes in the back of his head, and he fooled many with his outrageous sense of humor. Little did they know, it was one of his most important survival skills. His wife blew him a kiss. He grabbed the kiss right before it reached his rear end. He put it in his mouth, pretended to eat it, and licked his fingers one by one, clean. The entire tribelet was now into the game, laughing and smiling.

"Just before dusk, most of the children carried their baskets to pick berries just outside the village. The beautiful, young woman-girl picked berries next to the boy with the shark-tooth necklace. He began to feel nervous again. Though he tried to keep his composure, he began to breathe heavily and broke into a sweat. She looked at him again with her seductive eyes. Suddenly, he felt dizzy and short of breath. Everything went black, and he fainted. He awoke to his mother fanning his face. He seemed to be in a daze.

She wept, as her husband sat, praying. The woman-girl ran under a tree and began to cry. Her mother followed her to comfort her. She knew about her daughter's love for the boy. She gently took hold of her daughter's chin and wiped away the tears. She then kissed her on top of her forehead and held her close. She was not ready to lose her baby to the arms of another.

"The Shaman stabbed his prayer stick into the ground. He then arranged mussels outside the camp as an offering. Then he put on his bear-claw necklace; colorful feathers surrounded the grizzly claw, which rested on the Shaman's chest. He reached for his deer-skin pouch, full of grizzly bear teeth. He sat down and opened the bag, sifting through the shiny yellow teeth with his chunky fingers as he drifted into a deep meditation."

Dennis slipped into a trance-like state, as if he were the Shaman. His words became thick, and his voice deepened.

"Moments later, the Shaman found himself transported from the camp at the beach to the base of a giant redwood tree, where he sat. Deep sounds of a grizzly bear filled the forest. Louder and louder, the moaning grew. Suddenly, the bear appeared directly behind the Shaman, reeking of the stench of fish. The Shaman remained still, trusting in this powerful animal. Then he turned around and looked the bear in the eye and merged into its body. He let out the loudest growl of all; the echo startled every bird in the forest, causing them to fly in mass out of the trees."

Dennis let out a roar that shook the room. The class screamed, and Randy held onto his desk.

"Jesus Christ!" he yelled.

"Amen, Brother!" Bliss replied, thinking Randy was actually calling upon Jesus, rather than cursing.

As Dennis continued to tell his story, his voice quivered with excitement, and his breathing became labored. It was as if the bear's energy streamed through him.

"The bear began running through the forest, snapping tree branches and underbrush. Breathing heavily and growling fiercely, he slowed down and walked until he reached a clearing. Two people stood there, embraced in a kiss. The bear ducked behind thick bushes, watching. It was the boy with the shark necklace and the woman-girl. She tickled the boy, teasing him and running away. He laughed and followed her. Their bodies faded away. The Shaman awoke from his experience.

"The Shaman looked over to the woman-girl, who sat under the tree, holding her mother. He then looked over to the tule hut where the sick boy lay, his father in deep prayer. The Shaman walked to the tule hut. Standing in front of the entrance, he stared at the boy's mother as she caressed her son's forehead. Color had returned to the boy's face.

"Then, the Shaman broke out into laughter. The mother looked at her son and back to the Shaman again. She got up, intending to yell at the Shaman for laughing at such a dire moment. He put his arm around her and pointed to the woman-girl, who was peacefully resting under the tree. The woman-girl looked toward the hut and saw the boy standing behind his mother and the Shaman.

"When the boy gazed at the woman-girl this time, he looked with different eyes. Now he was tall-boy, ready for woman-girl. He walked over to her and sat down. Her mother slowly walked away. This pairing signaled the end of the age of innocence and the beginning of a cycle of love that endured for centuries."

ELEVEN

Viper slipped back into the room through the backdoor and sat down in his chair.

"Where in the hell have you been? I can't believe you just left me like that," Holly said.

Viper's hair was wet and his eyes were bloodshot.

"What's wrong with you?" Holly asked.

Dennis welcomed him back with a nod, while Ms. Rowanna gave him a stern look. Viper knew not to say a word as Dennis spoke again.

"As the sun sank into the horizon, the tribelet arrived at their main campsite at Lighthouse Field, carrying baskets of berries and fish. The leader greeted them with hugs. Everyone was laughing, hugging, and kissing.

"Mothers wrapped their babies in handwoven blankets, deer-skin, or rabbit-skin capes as people gathered around the fire. The women formed two teams to gamble around the fire. Each team laid out their beaded necklaces, fur coats, and shells. The game began as one team fell into a rhythmic dance. Everyone's atten-tion turned toward the Shaman's wife, with her thick, round face. Each team aimed to convince the other that their "magic trick" was real. Several women on the team drummed a simple rhythm, which became faster and faster as the Shaman's wife spun around and around. Without warning, her face turned into that of an eagle, and fire spewed from her mouth, completing her performance. Her team roared with support: Surely, the other team could not top this.

"Then Woman-Girl got up. Slowly and seductively, she danced through the merchandise, so carefully laid out in front of the women, as if it were already hers. The drums pounded louder and so did her heartbeat. She disrobed, and her body shone, radiant, from head to toe. She captivated everyone's attention, including Tall-Boy's.

"The sound of her heartbeat grew louder and louder, until it was all anyone could hear. She let out a visceral scream, and two white doves emerged from her chest as she collapsed to the ground.

"One by one, the women quietly covered her with all of their possessions. It was clear her team had won. Tall-Boy stood with tears in his eyes. He knew then he would have two children with her.

"The next morning, as the sun rose, the Shaman faced east, giving thanks for a new day. Tall-Boy and his fellow huntsmen joined in, to bless their hunt. On their way out of the village camp, they passed a group of children lying on the grassy terrain. As they gazed at the sky, they tickled one another's forearms. The youngest hunter kept his eyes on the children as they passed, wondering whether he was ready to become a man. An elder whistled, signaling him to hurry. Reluctantly, he ran to catch up with the group.

"The hunters surrounded a meadow, hiding in the surrounding tall grasses. An antelope came out of the woods, into the open grass to graze.

"As they crept closer and closer, the animal moved farther and farther away. Finally, one of the huntsmen managed to get close to the antelope. He rolled over on his back and kicked his legs and arms up into the air. The animal cautiously moved toward the man, sniffing, looking around him, stopping and moving in even closer. Then the man became still.

"As they carried the dead antelope home, Tall-Boy led the group. It had been a successful day, and the younger boy brought up the rear with pride. He carried a dozen rodents, their bodies hanging from a stick, swung over his shoulder.

"The leader heard the huntsmen's horn, signaling their return, as he sat in his large tule with his three wives. While the men passed through the village, women worked, sang, and prepared for their feast. The leader's wives remained in the tule as he escorted the men to the river to bathe. The young boy skipped past the working women, nonchalantly displaying his rodent prizes. They cheered for him as he walked into the arms of his mother. He handed her the stick and ran off to bathe with his elders at the river.

"During the feast, the tribe danced and sang around the fire. They didn't notice when Tall-Boy disappeared into the forest with Woman-Girl.

"Not even ten moons later, Tall-Boy paced outside of Woman-Girl's hut. Everyone tended to the woman giving birth, and they looked worried. Every time she let out a cry, the children clung to their mothers. Then the sun set, and the stars came out. By this time, almost everyone huddled close together at the great fire—everyone except Tall-Boy and the Shaman.

"The Shaman eventually convinced Tall-Boy to leave the entrance of the hut and go into the sweathouse, where they could cleanse and pray until the arrival of his child.

"More men joined Tall-Boy, humming and chanting as they perspired out fears of evil spirits that might want to take the newborn. The sounds of the woman in labor faded as their songs grew louder and louder. Everyone outside could hear the music emanate from the sweat lodge. Hand in hand, they circled around the birthing hut, swaying to the rhythm of the music.

"Emotions vacillated from fearful to hopeful, until they heard the first cry of the baby. Everyone relaxed, and Tall-Boy ran over to the hut, where the new mother rested peacefully with the baby.

His beautiful wife had a glow around her as she held their newborn baby. The baby's face wrinkled, so tiny and helpless in his mother's arms, as she guided his little lips to her breasts.

"Moments later, Tall-Boy heard another cry, different than his newborn's, but a newborn cry, nonetheless.

"'What could that be?' Tall-Boy wondered.

"With tears in her eyes, the Shaman's wife held the twin so Tall-Boy could see. Not only did the Great Spirit give him one child, but two. His heart swelled with joy.

"The Shaman remained in the sweat lodge with the others, singing loudly, nodding his head up and down, and chuckling. He didn't need to walk over to the hut to see the twins. Overhead, two falling stars appeared over a full moon, and a coyote cried out."

TWELVE

By this time, Viper had settled down, into his angry self. "Oh, my God. It's the neverending story…"

Holly sunk into her chair, avoiding eye contact—and any association—with him. Ms. Rowanna wrote up a referral to the principal but intended to wait until after class to deliver it to him.

"What a rude kid," she thought to herself. "I can just imagine his parents."

Randy and Eric both looked back at him. He stared at them with his piercing dark eyes. "His eyes look like black holes," Eric thought to himself. Randy tried to remember when they first met and wondered why he never played at Viper's house.

"I don't even remember when he moved here," he thought to himself.

Despite Viper's comment, Dennis remained determined to finish his story before the bell rang.

"August 28, 1791, was a windy and foggy day. A lone priest, wrapped in several pounds of gray-colored, tattered robes, pounded a huge wooden cross into the dirt, then dropped to his calloused knees and prayed. On September 25, 1791, three exhausted priests arrived to what is now known as Santa Cruz on mules, followed by a mule train of supplies and livestock. One of them pointed to the cross with excitement.

"'There it is! We have arrived at last! Oh, dear Father, you have heard our cries. You have not led us astray. God bless the holy cross, in the name of the Father, and the Son and the Holy Ghost. Amen.'"

"Yes! God bless and amen," Jade and Bliss simultaneously shouted. Stunned that they had both spoken the same words at the same time, they giggled. Dennis smiled at them.

"Little did we know we had many visitors cross our paths who had been claiming our land for years. Cabrillo, Drake, Vizcaino, and the Portola party. Cortez led an expedition back in 1535, to Baja California, which opened a path to establish its chain of missions. There were twenty-one missions in all. Santa Cruz was twelfth on the list.

"The first priests built a Catholic Church, considering themselves Utopian visionaries. They planned to convince the 'savages' to serve a ten-year apprenticeship. During this time, we 'savages' would learn to live like 'civilized' people. We would first and foremost become baptized and live according to the white man's faith. We would learn to read, write, speak their language, pray properly, eat with tools, wear clothing, and master farming, masonry, and other civilized duties. When the ten years were up, we would be given our own little pieces of land so the missionaries could move on to save other souls in need."

"Yes, amen, amen," Jade blurted out.

Dennis smiled once again, patiently. He knew the girls had a long way to go before they understood the story.

"One night, the three priests ate around a campfire. They heard a noise in a nearby bush. One priest tried to comfort the others, telling the men it was probably a deer."

"Yeah, it was a deer or something! Maybe it was the devil," Viper interrupted again.

"That's it," Ms. Rowanna said. "That will be enough. One more time and you are going straight to the office."

Dennis put his hand up to stop the disturbance in the room.

"Of course, even the priest did not believe a deer made the sound. He didn't want to know what it was. The rustling sound continued to come from bushes, then ended with an unidentifiable scream—unlike any animal or human could make.

"'Oh Lord save us,' one of the priests cried out."

Viper laughed wickedly.

"Though the priests remained unharmed," Dennis continued, "they barely slept all night. They huddled together, like children cuddling."

The class laughed at the thought of priests sleeping together.

"The next day, at the Ohlone camp, a young man ran into the campsite, screaming. He upset everyone, as he told them about the three men he saw when he was hunting. He didn't have the words to describe the priests—he didn't even know the word 'priest,' and he certainly wasn't familiar with the clothing they wore and the animals that accompanied them. He wasn't even sure whether they were human. None of them had any hair on their heads. He thought that maybe they came from the sky, like the ones that fly with feathers.

"Not too long afterward, the priests showed up on their mules. They were dressed in long gray robes with a simple tie around their waists. They stopped in the middle of the village, and a small child peeked out of her hut. The priests began to play peek-a-boo with the child, as other villagers cautiously peered from their huts.

"Then the leader appeared, his shoulders held back in pride, to greet these gray-cloaked, hairless creatures from the vast sky. He studied the sky creatures and even sniffed them, but he could not identify their look or smell; they seemed puffy and smelled slightly of musk. The priests stared at the leader with equal intrigue: They had heard stories about the 'savages.'

"After sizing up each other, the priests cautiously pulled out beaded necklaces, with crosses dangling in the middle of them. They extended the strange-looking necklaces to the leader, and he took them. The leader recognized the profitable trading that could take place. In exchange, he offered them stringed shells and invited them into his hut, where they ate and drank. Meanwhile, the rest of the tribe worked quietly and diligently as they prepared for a huge feast for their newfound friends. But while the villagers welcomed the strange men, the Shaman stared out at the river in a trance-like state. Tears flowed from his eyes; he could see the impending doom.

"The priests seemed to get along with everyone—everyone except the Shaman and his wife, who knew of the Shaman's vision. When the sun fell and the stars rose with the moon, the Shaman built a great fire as he chanted prayers to his guides, in hopes of saving his people. He was the first one to dance, intending to scare off the priests, while his wife sang in a prayer trance near the fire. Many of the tribesmen joined in the Shaman's uncharacteristic behavior, believing he knew something they did not. The scene disturbed the leader, and he immediately called for a meeting in his hut. The Shaman remained by the fire.

"'Surely these people come from the mule,' the tribesmen thought of the priests. 'They look just like that strange animal, the mule, with their matching gray robes. Who are they, and what do they want? Will they move on when trading is finished? Why is their skin that color? Why is Shaman trying to scare them away? Are they sick? Are they cursed?'

"These and many more questions remained unanswered that fateful night. The Shaman did not know exactly what danger lay ahead, but he knew it was not good. He didn't care what they bought or traded; he just wanted them to leave. The Shaman blew a handful of dusty herbs toward the priests' eyes, and the sky began to roar. Thunderous clouds covered the heavens and blocked the moonlight. Lightning lit up the entire sky. The music of the Indians grew as the beat got louder and louder."

Once again, the classroom grew dark as clouds formed outside. Lightning struck and rattled the windows. Some students ducked their heads under their desks.

"Suddenly, the Shaman could see past his village: Over a hill, down by the San Lorenzo River and out of a thick foggy bank, the Indian who had been murdered at the river appeared on land. His long black hair flew around his head, his eyes glowed red, and his face looked foreboding, heavily made up in war paint. He thrashed wildly and let out a screech that was not human, not animal. Then, the fog enveloped him, and he disappeared back into the river."

Viper sat nervously, gripping his pant legs and breathing heavily. "Why are you acting so weird?" Holly asked him.

He didn't answer.

THIRTEEN

The weather outside the classroom cleared up again. Dennis was determined to finish his story before the bell rang. The class cooperated, mesmerized. Never before had Ms. Rowanna seen high school students sit so attentively. But then again, neither had she ever brought in Dennis before.

"Weeks later," Dennis continued, "well beyond the village, a mission bell rang as the sun crept up over a mountaintop. A soldier marched down the church's hallway, unlocking and pounding on all of the thick wooden doors to wake up the Indians. As the Indians came out of their barren rooms, cows grazed in a grassy field surrounding the area. The entire tribe now lived at the mission site. A group of them went to work, bending wet clay over their thighs to create tiles for the roof. Others carried bricks, stacked on wooden slabs and balanced above their heads.

"The women learned to weave, sew, and cook—the European way. Woman-Girl collected eggs from penned-up chickens. Her twins played with some of the chicks in their laps. Shaman's wife found herself face-to-face with a sheep. He bleated, and she bleated back.

"Everyone walked with heads hung low. No one smiled or made eye contact with anyone else. The children learned to read and write and studied Christianity with the priests. One mother spent most of her days weeping in the corner of the half-built mission, rocking her toddler on her lap.

"With the mission came more Spaniards. They forced my people to move into the mission and help them build it with soldiers they rounded up from Mexico. My people became imprisoned slaves. The priests baptized my ancestors one by one, saying they were saving their souls. If my people tried to escape or refused to study, soldiers beat them in front of everyone.

"One day, a priest was teaching a group of men to read the Bible. He read aloud, and then tried to get Tall-Boy to sound out the words. Tall-Boy looked at him with confusion. The priest repeated the words, over and over again. Animosity built as Tall-Boy refused to respond. The priest grew impatient, got up and yelled at him. Tall-Boy laid his head on the table and covered his ears. Tall-Boy's father, who sat next to him, stood up and threw the Bible across the room. This started an angry stare-down between the priest and the Indian.

"Then the Shaman stood up. One by one, they all stood up to join proudly in the stare-down. The priest felt surrounded and fearfully backed out of the room. Later, he beat Tall-Boy's father. Everyone was required to watch."

As Bliss started to cry, Jade comforted her.

"In the beginning, there were eighty-nine Indians living at the mission and only four soldiers and one corporal. The Indians were separated from loved ones, including wives, husbands, and children. Men and women remained segregated. Tall-Boy and Woman-Girl tried to cling to each other, but the soldiers ripped them apart. The twins held onto their father as long as they could, as soldiers dragged him away.

"Woman-Girl screamed and fell to her knees. Shaman extended his arms out to his wife. With their palms touching, tears welled up in their eyes. Then the soldiers dragged him away. Many times the soldiers locked up the 'heathens,' as they called them, in isolation. They separated villagers to control them. One day, they escorted the Shaman to a small room, in which Catholic trinkets decorated the walls. In the middle of one wall, a huge painted cross took center stage. A soldier shoved the Shaman into the room, and then he threw a Bible at him before locking the door.

"Within a couple of years, they ultimately killed us off—it began little by little, one by one, until it spread from tribe to tribe. They destroyed every village from San Diego to San Francisco.

"And for what? Land? Money? Power? How about all of it. Spain demanded colonization, so the soldiers detained or destroyed anyone in their way. They managed to maim and tame most of the Indian Nation in Mexico and force the tribesmen into military duties before they worked their way up to Santa Cruz. They took our spirit, and they replaced it with Bibles."

"Prison life was just the beginning of the misery. European diseases swept through the missions: measles, mumps, small pox, influenza, and syphilis. Many became too sick to work.

"The women and children were the first to go: Several women and children lived together in a small room. As they fell ill, one by one, healthy women tended to the ailing's needs. Woman-Girl's face and arms broke out in red bumps and sores, and then her twins caught the disease.

"When she discovered one of them lifeless in her arms, she began to scream, while others wept and pounded on the locked door, begging for help. Shaman's wife rose to comfort Woman-Girl. She, too, was dying."

Jade started to cry, and Bliss couldn't comfort her much because she was also distraught. It was all too much. Ms. Rowanna passed around a box of Kleenex and blew her nose loudly.

Dennis wiped his eyes before continuing.

"Several men lived in the small room next door. Tall-Boy was sick also. He put his ear up against the wall and heard Woman-Girl bemoan the death of their daughter. Tall-Boy slid helplessly down to his knees and began to weep. His eyes blurred as he looked at the corner of the room, where the men had built a memorial to the Shaman with the few belongings he had. He had passed days prior.

"On average, six Indians died for every birth. It took less than two decades to eradicate the natives.

"After that, Spanish and Mexican soldiers raided the Yokuts and many other Central Valley tribes and forced them to work at the mission.

"We lost our people, our land, our culture, and our language. We lost our heritage, and some of us even lost our minds.

"Twenty-one years later, in 1812, something very strange happened. A messenger arrived at the mission and sent the priest out into the night. He told the priest someone was dying in a nearby orchard.

"This particular priest had a reputation for throwing fits of rage and abusing women. He looked upon the Indians as filthy, dirty beings who were not cooperating in the establishment of his Catholic Utopia. Whether his anger stemmed from things not going his way or from the possibility that he was an extra bad seed doesn't matter: He was just a little more than everyone could take.

"When the priest arrived at the dark orchard, he could only see the moon and an outline of a tree. A coyote howled and startled the priest. Then the night quieted—until he heard the screams. They were not like those of an animal. They were something else entirely."

Once again, Viper started clenching his pants legs.

"Why does he keep going on and on like this?" he asked Holly.

"Why do you keep going on and on like this?" she replied. "You are being so weird. Like, I don't even know you."

Howard looked over at Randy. Randy's face reminded him of the bathroom incident.

"Was everyone possessed or what?" Howard wondered. Giliano glanced at Howard and pushed his glasses off the end of his nose.

Dennis remained spellbound by his story as he continued to speak.

"The blood-curdling sounds made the priest's hair stand straight up along the back of his neck. He could hear drumming, first distant, then louder, as if it moved closer and closer to him. Suddenly, the image of an Indian came into focus. The wind remained still, yet his long black hair flew around his head. His eyes glowed red and deep, and his face stood out, painted war-like. The image faded in and out of focus, as if taunting him.

"'Who are you? What do you want?' asked the desperate man.

"The ghost revealed himself fully, but not even he was aware of what was to happen next.

"'No, please. Oh, oh Lord Jesus Christ, oh it hurts so badly. Please stop! You're hurting me; please stop. Please.'"

The entire class sat on the edge of their seats. Ms. Rowanna held a wad of Kleenex, squeezed into the size of a tennis ball.

"No one ever found out exactly happened to him that night," said Dennis.

"The next morning, the priest was lying on his bed. The soldiers had to break the door down to reach him. He was dead.

"The soldiers unlocked and searched all of the Indians' rooms, only to find nothing. Someone had to take the blame. But whom?

"Pogonip, the river ghost, raged: Rows and rows of dead Indians lined up, side by side, on the riverbank. Pogonip, the lost soul, swore to seek revenge for his people and his land forever.

"The soldiers didn't know how the Indians escaped from their locked rooms, how the priest died, and how the Indians locked themselves back in their rooms, as if nothing happened. One old Indian, who survived the massacre, was whipped as his young grandson was forced to watch. No one knows exactly what happened. It is this, and many other questions, that have never been answered."

FOURTEEN

The bell rang, startling the students. It felt like Dennis had hypnotized them, bringing them through hundreds of years in just one hour. Many of the students' eyes were red from crying. Bliss and Jade held their heads low in confusion. "How could our ancestors have been responsible for this abuse?" they wondered. Ms. Rowanna felt shaky and straightened her skirt in an attempt to compose herself.

"Wow. What can I say?" she replied to Dennis. "I, I, feel like I was there. Thank you, Dennis."

Viper strutted up to Dennis.

"Thank you very much. I knew I wasn't crazy. The curse of Santa Cruz—it's real. What an amazing experience," he said as he let out a cynical laugh. "I can't wait to see what's going to happen next!"

Ms. Rowanna sternly handed Viper a slip. "Take this to the office, young man."

He grabbed it out of her hand and sneered at her.

Leslie walked up to Dennis and gave him a big hug. She glared at Viper and said, "We were there: all of us."

Viper shook his hands defensively and craned his neck. "Ooooh, I'm scared," he said.

Leslie ignored him.

"Thank you, Uncle Dennis."

Eric stopped in his tracks, and Ms. Rowanna was amazed, as well.

"Dennis is your uncle?" asked Ms. Rowanna.

Leslie had a big smile on her face.

"I didn't want to say anything and disrupt the class. I knew he had a lot to cover in a short time. But I had no idea he was going to tell the whole story!"

"Her mother is my sister-in-law," Dennis said. "Her great-grandmother taught me everything I know."

"Well, I've got to get to my next class," Leslie said. "I love you, Uncle Dennis!"

Eric followed Leslie, saying under his breath: "I love you too, Leslie."

But Randy dragged him in the other direction. Leslie looked back as she walked away and flashed him a little grin. Randy temporarily interrupted Eric's concentration on Leslie.

"Can you believe that old man? What a trip! And what was up with the bear face?"

Eric didn't recall any bear face. "Bear face? What are you talking about?"

Randy suddenly felt self-conscious, thinking maybe he had imagined too much into Dennis' story.

"Never mind," Randy said. "Dude, let's surf right after practice today. Daylight savings is almost spent."

Eric's attention lingered upon Leslie. He smiled back at her just before she turned away. Then Holly and Viper passed by. Randy shot off his mouth, as usual, to Holly.

"I need some sexual healing."

Viper answered this time.

"Then why don't you do what you do best and go home and whack off?"

Randy shoved Viper, and Viper shoved him back. Eric got in-between them.

"Is this how it's going to be all year, again? When are you two going to grow up?"

Eric stormed off.

Randy and Viper stood there in a staring contest, their heads slightly swaying from left to right like those of roosters. Tim walked up. He had his eye on them all along. "Is everything cool here, boys? Or am I going to have to take you downtown? The principal won't put up with any kung-fu fighting this year. Do not pass go; do not collect two hundred dollars—it's straight to jail this time. Got it, grasshoppers?"

Randy threw a fit.

"I don't know who's worse, you or him! I'm outta here!" Tim saw the referral slip in Viper's hand and grabbed it.

"Oh, what's this? Looks like we need to take little walk down the hall. Let's go."

"Thank God," said Holly. "Please take him."

She had seen a side of Viper that day that she never wanted to see again. She was tired of people in her life who didn't act right. "Why can't everyone just be normal?" she mumbled, irritated. She was growing weary of being in a committed relationship with such a creep with so many secrets.

FIFTEEN

After finishing football practice, the boys ran into the locker room to strip down from their sweaty jerseys and jump in the cold shower.

Randy was pumped.

"Are we going to catch some waves or what? I heard it's going off. Huge swell. Unheard of for September, dude!"

Eric didn't feel as excited, and he wasn't sure exactly why. Randy was still his best friend and all. Eric was just getting sick of all of the bull crap: And Randy didn't give him much respect—probably because Randy didn't have any respect for himself, he figured. The friendship was getting expensive. Eric could feel himself pulling away from Randy.

"I'll get wet, but I have a lot of homework."

Thomas was always odd-man-out for some reason. No one really gave it any thought, except for Thomas. Deep down, he knew it was his own doing: He loved hanging with the boys, but he knew they both were somewhat of a bad influence. He worked too damn hard for anything to slow him down with his studies or his future. But the fact was, he still wanted buddies to hang out with.

"What's Rowanna's class like?"

Randy was cocked and ready to fire.

"Just a bunch of freaks, man. You wouldn't believe it. Especially Rowanna. I really don't know how to describe it. She's just kind of large-headed and hairy. And they're actually talking about the curse! Jesus!"

Eric couldn't even think about the curse. He had one thing on his mind and one thing only: Leslie.

"How's the new chick, Leslie?" It was as if Thomas had read Eric's mind.

"I want to get her in the back and yum, finger-licking good," Eric said. "I've just gotta have me some of that."

Suddenly, Thomas' southern drawl kicked in. His parents came from the deep South. They came from a long line of hardworking, kick-ass slaves, literally. Thomas was well aware of where he came from and where he was going. When he was out of his comfort zone, he would regress into a homie accent real quick, out of defense. His voice was a little higher pitched, and he spoke much faster than usual.

"What up with the curse? Is that fo' real?"

"Come on, man," Randy said. "That's the stupidest thing I ever heard of. A curse? Give me a break!"

"I don't know, man," Eric stepped in. "There were some freaky things that happened in the '70s."

The statement irritated Thomas. He had no idea anything bad ever happened in Santa Cruz—in the beautiful little city his mom and dad once called "The Promised Land." For them, it held the promise of a carefree, liberated, unadulterated society, which they called home.

"Really? Like what?"

Thomas wasn't sure he really wanted to know, but the words just came out. Eric had dried off and begun to chew on a hangnail that had been bothering him all day.

"Oh. You don't remember?" he said.

Thomas laughed nervously. "Uh, not exactly. We weren't born yet, remember?

"Just tell him already," Randy said, impatiently.

They tightened their damp towels around their waists and sat down on the wooden benches. Eric began the story of the serial killers.

SIXTEEN

"It was a warm October afternoon in 1970, a time when my parents say American youths questioned the standards and expectations of society as a whole. With the senseless Vietnam War in full-throttle and the crazy psychedelic drug phase, everyone just spoke their mind. People walked around nude and ignored the expectations of the American Dream our grandparents strived for. Apparently, Santa Cruz attracted a lot of people. It supported things like exploring the possibilities of out-of-body experiences. People came to Santa Cruz because it was just an hour or so south of San Francisco, the Mecca of the hippie culture craze and flower power. People lived on the leading edge of thought and expansion; poets and songwriters roamed the streets in torn and tattered jeans. Women burned their bras, and men grew their hair long. My parents said people shared the resources they had with 'peace' and love.' It was a time when people acted like 'anything goes.'

"No one knows exactly when the first hippies stepped foot in Santa Cruz. But around the time they came, bad things started to happen. No one knew if Santa Cruz suddenly experienced a wave of bad luck, or if it resulted from irresponsible and confused dropouts. Some people blame it on an eerie vortex, which Santa Cruz sits upon. And some blame it on the curse. Whatever the cause, heartbreak was about to strike the sleepy little town of Santa Cruz once again.

"One day, Don Findley Lazier was hiding out in the bushes, smoking a joint," Eric said.

Thomas interrupted.

"Who's that?"

"Oh, you'll see," Eric replied.

The last player on the team slammed his locker closed and shouted, "Later, boys," as the trio remained in the locker room.

"Okay, so there was this hippie guy hiding in the bushes of an expensive home," Eric continued. "He was smoking a joint. It was the guy I just said: Don Findley Lazier. He sat there laughing by himself, for no reason at all. Maybe it was because he was so high."

The boys in the locker room felt like they were being sucked back in time as Eric began the story of "The Murder Capital of the World."

"Don Findley thought to himself, 'Why am I laughing? Here I am on business and there's nothing funny about it.'

"He was there to make a statement about materialism. He was going to show the world why it was wrong to drive expensive cars and why it was wrong to live in a beautiful house and have expensive jewelry. He was going to make someone pay for the wrong turn America took when it began to lean on capitalism.

"'Someone with a lot of money who knew how to spend it is going to pay the ultimate price,' the stoner thought to himself. 'They'll pay with their lives, and then everyone will see how important it is to stop behaving like that.'

"And that's how it was going down. It seemed pretty simple in his mind.

"He wished he had enjoyed the easy life growing up, but he hadn't. His parents split up, and his mom had no money. When he was five, she had to give him up. He grew up in foster homes, but he ran away a lot.

"They tried to say he was crazy, but the way he saw it was: Crazy is what crazy did to him. People in the system took children into their homes for the wrong reasons. They were mean people, with perverted motives having to do with his lips and his behind. The abuse tied knots of hate into him, running from his heart to his brain. Just like Dennis talked about the priests breaking the natives' spirits, these people broke this guy's spirit. He never even connected why he had so many hateful thoughts, thoughts about killing people. He felt totally disconnected; he just wanted to kill the pain. It was all he could think about.

"That night, he decided to make it happen. He smoked to calm himself down, but rather than relaxing, he began giggling, and that angered him even more. It was as though his own mind became his worst enemy.

"'Why am I so fucking pissed off?' he thought to himself.

"He tried to ignore the thought. No one was going to ruin his perfect plan. He just wanted to tip someone off, help them understand why he had to carry out his plan and let them know it'd be a small price to pay for redemption.

"He waited until dark, when the fog rolled in, as usual. If he had his way, he'd eliminate the fog, too—it made it so damn hard to see.

"'Fucking fog.'

"He knew if he started obsessing about the fog, it'd fire him up too much.

"'Don't think about the fog. Don't think about the fog,' he repeated to himself.

"But his mind wouldn't stop. Every time he told himself not to think about the fog, it made him think of it even more. His own thoughts began to drive him crazy as they swirled around in his mind. He hated being a genius, always thinking about everything. He convinced himself another couple of drags would set him straight, but in reality, it sent him further off the deep end.

"The smoke coiled around his thick, bushy beard and rolled slowly up his nostrils as he reviewed his plan. Some time passed—he didn't know how much—and he ended up in a backyard, stoned out of his skull, without any recollection of how he got there. But he remembered his plan.

"'Stick to the plan,' he told himself. 'In and out.'

"His heartbeat pounded like that of a wolf chasing a rabbit.

"'Try not to enjoy it too much. This is strictly business,' he said aloud to himself. 'But they do deserve to feel it. And feel it real good, too.'

"He wanted them to feel the pain they caused the earth by purchasing worldly items for themselves—those sons of bitches. They contributed to the death cycle of the planet.

"'I owe it to them,' he said, making no sense at all.

"'Yeah, I'm right on track. I'm going in for the kill. It's now or never.'

"Ever so quietly, he snuck through an open screen door, leading into the master suite of the Zhengs' home. There he found Mrs. Zheng. She liked the finer things in life, and she wore them well. He had watched her, targeted her for a long time, and now he hid in the shadows of her walk-in closet. Days before, he had walked into the Zhengs' home and stolen a pair of binoculars, using them to spy on the family from the bushes on the hillside. Now Mrs. Zheng stood right in front of him.

"As she stepped out of the shower, he gazed at her back, so smooth and silky as it shimmered with beads of water. A towel covered her midriff as she propped up one leg on the counter to rub in lotion. It smelled like cocoa butter, a smell he loved because it reminded him of the long, warm summer days he spent at the beach when he was a small child.

"He almost turned away and scrapped the plan. He still had time. No one would have known how close she came to death. But his obsession urged him to move on with the plan, so he approached her. Her thick blonde hair shone like a halo around her head. It was so beautiful; he wished he were frying on acid.

"'Now that would be a real trip,' he thought to himself.

"A few brightly colored scarves hanging on the closet door caught his attention. Then he looked back at her. She had finished applying the lotion, and she looked in the mirror. She reminisced about swimming in the pool earlier with her family, then her thoughts turned to what she would make for dinner as she brushed her hair.

"He came up so quickly behind her that she didn't have time to scream. Shrills of fear ran up her spine, tingling into her scalp. Her whole body sounded an internal alarm. Her heart pounded so hard that it literally felt as if it were going to explode through her chest. He shoved his finger up to her mouth, saying, 'Don't scream—or else.'

"She hoped if she remained quiet, maybe he wouldn't hurt her. She began to shake uncontrollably, and in a terrified whisper, she asked, 'What do you want?'

"Her legs felt like jelly—she didn't know how much longer she could hold herself up. He told her everything was going to be fine, but he knew they were only words, words so easily spoken by a predator. She froze, too scared to cry. He stood behind her, solidly gripping her neck. She felt like prey, like an animal fighting for its life. He asked where she kept her jewelry. She led him to it.

"'Put it on,' he said.

"'Which piece?' she muttered as her shaking hands reached to open the oversized case.

"'All of it,' he replied.

"She began to put on all of her jewelry: the Rolex watch, the Bulgari earrings, the Tiffany and Harry Winston rings, the Buccellati necklace, the Choppard, the Van Cleef and Arpels bracelets.

"Her lower lip trembled as she began to cry. To an outsider, she would have looked like a little girl caught with mommy's jewelry. But to him, she looked like the King of England in drag. Tears ran down her long lashes to her cheeks. She felt devastated; she knew there was no way out. He pushed her over to the hanging scarves and grabbed a handful of them.

"'Which one is your favorite color?' he asked calmly.

"'Red,' she responded, too scared not to. 'I like the red one best.'

"He bound her hands together with the red scarf.

"'And which perfume is your favorite?' he asked.

"She stared at him for what seemed like an eternity. She hoped her husband would walk in and save her. Surely someone would come, she thought, trying to gather herself together, if she could just stall him.

"'Uh, um, I like Yves St. Laurent. It's over there.'

"She cocked her head toward a shelf near her vanity, hoping he didn't find it right away. His eyes scanned the shelf, but he couldn't figure out which one was the Yves St. Laurent. There were at least twenty bottles.

"'Jesus, lady, you think you have enough perfume bottles? Fuck it.'

"He gathered a bunch in his arms and slammed them on the marble floor right in front of her. Then he grabbed the remaining bottles, one at a time, and sprayed her entire body, until it dripped with the pungent smell of mixed colognes and perfumes. He squirted the last spray directly into her eyes. She hardly felt the sting; by now, her eyes swelled with pain from sobbing. Suddenly, her husband walked in the back door. Don hushed the woman, pulling a gun on her.

"'Call him up here,' he demanded. She obeyed.

"As soon as Dr. Zheng stepped foot in the room, Don shoved Mrs. Zheng into the corner of the closet and pointed the gun at her husband.

"'Well, hello there, Dr. Zheng. Your wife and I were just playing a game; I'm glad you could join us,' he said, pushing the doctor into the closet where the scarves hung. 'Please be so kind as to choose your favorite color.'

"Dr. Zheng looked over at his wife, shaking in the corner. Her wide eyes, brimming with tears, let him know this man meant business.

"'Black,' Dr. Zheng answered, and within seconds, the man tied the doctor's hands so tight he might as well have been pinned in a straightjacket.

"Within an hour, Don had lured the entire family into the master bedroom and tied them up with colorful scarves. Everyone, including the couple's two sons and the maid, ultimately ended up floating dead in the pool, their hands tied with a rainbow of scarves.

"He had shot each one in the head, except for Dr. Zheng, whom he had shot twice in the back and once under the arm. He had no choice: Once Dr. Zheng chose his color, the doctor fell into a complete rage and tried to grab the gun. But he was no match for the crazy man.

"As Dr. Zheng lay on the ground in his own warm pool of blood, he saw some figures in a light as he was gently lifted out of his body. At first, he wondered, 'What was that light, who were those people, and where was he going?' But he soon knew that everything was going to be okay. No, better than okay. He beamed with love in his heart. He could feel his soul flying. He surrendered like a bird in flight when he saw the faces of the people he recognized in the warmth of this brilliant light, to which he was undeniably drawn. He saw his wife and children. They reached out their hands to him as his heart filled with complete and utter love. They were going home.

"After the slaying, Don busied himself making an even more dramatic statement; he lit the house on fire and moved Dr. Zheng's Rolls Royce in front of the driveway to block the entrance.

"'One last thing,' he thought. 'Glad I didn't forget. This was all easier than I thought it would be. What would the world be without me? I can't wait till the press gets hold of this. Then everyone is gong to know what I know. I should be getting paid for this. Wait a second. Fuck that. I don't care about money. That's the whole reason I did it. What in the hell is wrong with me? But I do deserve to get paid for it. It was a pain in the ass. Now I have to go and find somewhere to wash my shirt.'

"But he didn't leave soon enough: As he tried to figure out where to clean up, the fire department came screeching down the street, followed by the police. The police handcuffed Don Findley Lazier. On his court date, he yelled at the reporters and cameras. He knew it would be his first chance to tell everyone what he did and why. He felt so confident about the righteousness of his actions that he literally thought the justice system would release him—quite quickly, actually—once they heard his story and came to their senses.

"'Today World War III will begin, initiated by the people of the free universe!' he yelled toward the cameras. 'From this day forward, anyone who misuses the natural environment or destroys it will suffer the penalty of death by the people of the free universe!'

"But things didn't work out according to his plan. He remained stuck in prison. He spent the rest of his life jailed and eventually hung himself. His last thought was, 'What in the hell was I thinking?'"

SEVENTEEN

Randy and Thomas totally freaked out on the story. Thomas stood up in front of the lockers, amazed.

"Where did you get all of this information?"

But Eric wasn't finished.

"I'll tell you when I am done."

They all huddled a little closer. It was spooky in the locker room when no one else was there, and hearing the story made it even worse.

"On October 13, 1972, Martin Hullen came to town to visit his parents. He pulled over to give a ride to an alcoholic bum. Loud voices in his head insisted that the bum wanted to die, and they gave Martin permission to do so.

"He pulled over, led the bum out of the car, and bashed him in the head with a baseball bat. Blood splattered all over him. He tasted it around his mouth as he licked the warm, thin blood that circulated through the bum's veins only moments ago. He liked the flavor of gin, even if it was mixed with a little blood; the taste excited him. It felt powerful to take someone's life and send him or her back to where they came from. He wondered whether God really existed, or if the whole thing was a lie. The possibilities fascinated him. And there he stood: Part of the life and death situation. He knew he couldn't bring life into this world—at least not like a woman could—but he knew he could take life out of a human. It felt big—really big. He not only could kill people, but also, he would be the last thing they ever saw before they died. He enjoyed the rush immensely—so much so that it compelled him to do it again.

"'Just one more time,' he rationalized. 'Then I'll never do it again.'

"That night, Martin caught a beautiful young woman hitch-hiking. 'Oh, this is a good one. It'll really mean something this time.' He pulled over and let her in the car.

"She smiled at him, saying, 'Thanks for the ride, man.'

"He smiled back. 'Anytime,' he said.

"Immediately, thoughts rushed through his head: 'I think I'll cut her head off. I've always wanted to see what that would look like. Fuck. Why is this making me horny? Oh, God. Please save me. Save her. Why do I have to be the one to do this?'

"She reached in her purse and lit up a joint.

"'It's okay if I smoke in your car, isn't it?'

"Her nonchalant attitude threw him off-guard.

"'Ah, sure. How about some acid?' he replied.

"'I'm down! I've been so out of my head lately, it's just what the doctor ordered!'

"'What a coincidence,' he replied.

"'Why is that?' she asked.

"'Oh, the whole out-of-your head thing,' he chuckled. 'I guess we are just two heads thinking the same thing!'

"She laughed. 'Are you out of your head too?'

"'Oh, yeah, I suppose a lot of people might think that.'

"They both laughed even harder. But he knew exactly what he was laughing about. He had a plan, one that took them to a wooded area. There, he parked the car.

"Later, police found her decapitated. She was in fact, 'out of her head,' Martin thought, as he carried out his dirty work.

"On November 4th, All Souls Day, Martin parked outside of St. Mary's Catholic Church in Los Gatos. He burned a cigarette on his penis to see what it would feel like.

"'It really hurts like hell,' he thought to himself. But he loved the smell of burning flesh—especially his own. The voices told him to do it. He stuck the dark orange tip of the cigarette on it again, only longer this time. He watched it burn a hole in his shaft. It popped, sizzled, and split wide open. During it all, he gazed at gay porn, while the voices granted him permission to kill again. But this time, he didn't want to listen. He began to pray.

"'God, give me the strength never to kill again.'

"A Doors song came on the radio; the song 'The End' methodically soothed his mood.

"'Screw God. There is no God anyway.'

"Martin's face froze up as his lips tightened and pushed inward toward his teeth.

"'California was going to slip into the ocean, and people in Vietnam sacrificed their lives to make it not happen. All of those poor bastards who went to war died for us. They died for California,' he thought.

"He pulled up his pants and slipped inside the church, sight unseen. He fell on his knees before a huge altar of Jesus and several lit candles and began to pray.

"'Why do these people want me to kill them?' he asked Jesus. 'I don't get it. California is in good standing now.'

"He thought he was alone, but he wasn't. A priest sat nearby in a confessional booth. He could hear the priest, praying to be slaughtered.

"'Why me?' Martin thought. 'Thank you for the acid, God—if you are really there. Thank you for the pot, too. I would be insane without it.'

"He walked over to the confessional booth and tried to get in, but he couldn't dislodge the door. He jiggled and wiggled the little old wooden knob harder and harder. Finally, the priest opened the door. The bloodthirsty villain pulled out a hunting knife and stabbed the priest repeatedly. A parishioner walked into the church, witnessed the bloodbath, screamed, and then ran out.

"At first, doctors diagnosed Martin with schizophrenia. It seemed to make sense: He had bounced in and out of mental institutions for years. He even heard the voices telling him his victims wanted to be killed. The voices convinced him that the Vietnam War actually occurred as a sacrificial consequence to save California from caving into the Pacific Ocean.

"By January of 1973, Martin convinced himself that the only reason the voices compelled him to kill stemmed from his drug habit. So after a series of more killing sprees, he decided to track down an old acquaintance from high school, whom he had some dealings with and smoked a lot of pot with—back in the day.

"Martin finally found him after a lengthy search. He shot a bullet in the wife's head and repeatedly stabbed them both. He left a small child completely devastated.

"After that, he drove to another woman's house and killed her and her two children. Police found so many body parts that week that they lost track of how many lives Martin truly took.

"The city suffered other pointless murders between April and May of 1973, including those committed by Fred Temper, who turned himself in a few weeks after Martin's arrest. A jury convicted Fred of killing and mutilating eight women, including his own mother, whose head he placed on the mantel at her sea-cliff home.

"Joseph Todd Smith, known as the Trail Side Killer, also left a trail of women behind in the Santa Cruz mountains. Some escaped without ever knowing danger lurked beside them.

"One time, police found a beautiful female reporter bludgeoned and almost dead in the back of a shutdown hotel on Front Street, near the pier. They never solved the case, but they found evidence that she was raped, beaten repeatedly in the head, and left for dead. She lay in a coma at first and then awoke with amnesia, which lasted for years. When she snapped out of it, she couldn't remember a thing.

"These and countless senseless other acts of unbearable murder left horrifying effects on numerous families and the community at large.

"People wondered whether someone lurked in their bushes, just waiting to jump out and stab them. So many insane murders in Santa Cruz occurred that the district attorney made a public announcement calling Santa Cruz 'Murderville.'

"Later, the press called it the Murder Capital of the World, which made things worse. It left the residents riddled with fearful anticipation and confirmed everyone's biggest nightmare."

In the locker room, the boys were terrified. Thomas looked at his watch.

"Damn! I have to get out of here!"

"Where did you come up with all of this shit?" Randy asked, perturbed.

"My parents told me, once I was old enough," Eric replied. "Their friends actually knew family members directly related to the murders. It's all true, and it's all because of the curse."

The boys dressed as quickly as they could and bailed out of there.

"You know, you have a hell of an imagination, Eric," Thomas said as he left. "Remind me not to ask you for any more stories. My family came here for a new life—a good life. And I plan on living a long life. I don't need all of your negativity. It's totally stressing me out. Anyway, my dad has been on vacation, so I need to get home."

The truth was, Thomas' dad had taken off for a fishing trip and never came home. Thomas thought maybe his parents got into a fight, and his mom didn't want to tell him. Still, he wondered.

EIGHTEEN

Randy and Eric drove toward the cliffs to Steamer Lane; then they jumped out of the truck with surfboards tucked under their arms. They knew about the dangers of surfing the water there. The average water temperature remained in the fifties, so everyone needed a wetsuit. To make matters worse, the sea lions weighed, on average, eight hundred pounds, and they didn't like people encroaching on their territory. The sea otters looked cute and small compared to the other creatures, but they had long, sharp claws and teeth. It wasn't uncommon for them to chase people out of the water when they instinctively protected their small pups. When they felt threatened, they often clawed at surfboards—or the surfer himself.

Then there were the harbor seals and elephant seals. The average elephant seal weighed up to five thousand pounds. Within the ocean swam sunfish—some weighing over two thousand pounds, as well as humpback whales, blue whales, gray whales, and killer whales, all of which shared the water with the surfers and anyone else who dared enter the water. But blue sharks were the most common in Santa Cruz. People often paid with their lives to surf the Santa Cruz oceans.

Random sets of waves rushed in, and their height could measure an average of twenty feet with a good winter swell. But this afternoon, nothing was going to stop the boys from getting wet.

On their way over the cliffs, Leslie jogged past. Eric and Leslie's eyes met.

"How's it gong?" he asked.

"Great! I love the cliffs! I could jog for hours. We didn't have anything like this in Watsonville."

"Yeah, ahh…." Eric didn't know what else to say.

"So, you're a surfer?" Leslie asked.

"Well, I, uh…"

"See you tomorrow!" Leslie said, running off.

"Later!" Eric called after her, too late for her to hear.

He chased after Randy and jumped off the cliff with his board. They caught a few good ones, until Viper rode past and sprayed Randy in the face with saltwater. Randy caught the next one, bumping Viper off a little wave he caught on the inside. As Randy paddled his way back out to grab another one, he spotted something floating in the water and picked it up.

"What the…?"

Eric could have heard him a mile away.

"It's a foot!"

Randy instinctively threw it back into the water.

"What?"

Eric paddled over and dove for the object Randy had rejected. He felt something almost immediately and grabbed it.

"Holy crap! It's a foot!"

Eric threw it out, but it accidentally landed on his board. Randy paddled over to take a look at it.

"Shit! It is a foot, for sure."

They both just stared at it. Neither wanted to touch it again. But they knew they should bring the foot to the cops. "We have to take it in." Randy almost puked looking at it.

"I ain't touching that thing again."

Randy leaned over his board and dry heaved. He would have puked if he had any food in his system, but he had run from school, to football practice, and to surf.

"Just paddle it in on your board."

"Fine," Eric said, gagging.

"It smells really gross!"

They paddled as fast as they could back to the rocky cliffs, and then they crawled up with their boards, carefully balancing the foot on Eric's board. It seemed like an eternity, but they finally reached Randy's truck—the biggest, black monster ever made. Randy had worked hard for that truck ever since he was eleven, doing yard work, until he obtained his work permit, at fifteen. He had borrowed money from his cousin to buy the truck, which he hoped would make up for a part of him that was much smaller than normal.

They threw the foot in the back of the truck bed, and it made a hard, thumping sound. The sound startled them, but their adrenaline had kicked in, so they jumped in the front and took off.

"Dude, that's the sickest thing I have ever seen," Randy said, shaking.

"No shit—let's drop it off so we can get rid of it," said Eric.

NINETEEN

Inside the police department, a group of cops gathered at the counter. Apparently, they already knew about it. In fact, the first officer knew exactly whose foot it was.

"Yep, it's him," the officer said. "He's been missing for a couple of days now. African American. He was fishing off of the rocks on West Cliff. Uh huh, that's him all right. That White guy."

One of the cops said, "Is he white or African American?"

The first officer replied, "African American."

"Then why did you say it's 'that white guy?'"

"Because his name is White, asshole. Got it? Looks like shark chum now. I guess we're going to have to call his family. I wonder if they have Barbie-size caskets—that's all they'll need for the foot."

They all laughed, except for the boys who were in shock over not only finding the foot, but also hearing the cops' reactions.

"Better yet, just stick it in a shoebox! I wonder if they are on a budget!"

Even louder laughter.

"It smells like chum," the other cop said. "I don't want to be the one to do it, to make the call." Then he leaned over and puked.

"You boys did good, real good," the first officer said. "Glad to see you are staying out of trouble. Now go home. And don't say a word about this to anybody. Santa Cruz doesn't need the bad press."

"Yes, sir," the boys answered. But once outside the police station, Eric let off steam.

"Don't they have to take a sensitivity class to be cops? I wonder what else is going on that we don't know about."

"Well, if anyone knows, I guess it's you," Randy replied. "You seem to know about everything that's going on around here. Is there anything else you want to share with me—just to make sure I have some really good nightmares tonight?"

"What is that supposed to mean?"

"Nothing—just that Indian guy with the red eyes and the bear face, your serial killer stories, the foot: It's been a little overwhelming. I just want to chill."

TWENTY

Later, Randy smoked a joint and blew the smoke out of his bedroom window until his mother knocked on the door. He didn't want to talk to her; he locked his door for that very reason.

"Randy? Are you calling it a night?" she whispered through the door.

"Yeah, Mom; night."

"Night, darling. Sweet dreams. I love you."

He didn't answer back. He took another quick drag off the joint and held it in until he couldn't hold his breath for another second. He wanted to make the best of it. He coughed a little as he blew out the last puff and crawled into bed.

He got stoned a lot—and for good reason, as far as he was concerned. His life was just too hard, and he couldn't bear to feel the pain. He felt isolated and alone, and he kept a lot of secrets— secrets that weighed heavily on his heart and took a toll not only on his attitude, but also on his entire outlook on life. He didn't mean to be such a jerk, but he felt overwhelmed with problems and with just about everything that ever happened to him. Especially when his dad left. He thought about that day and its sequence of events. It was a day he couldn't wait to forget.

No longer had he drifted off to sleep than he found himself in a dream comparable to the day he had just experienced. He could hear Dennis, the Indian guy's voice from class, talking to him.

"On September 16, 1810, Mexico gained independence from Spain. All land grants were made under Mexican rule."

Dennis' voice was much clearer now. Randy tried to wake up from the dream, but he couldn't escape.

"For a short while, the Rancheros took total control of Santa Cruz—if 'control' is what you want to call it."

The dream transformed into a movie for Randy. And he was about to make his grand debut—as the lead actor. He could see himself at a ranch house. It was morning, in 1810. How he knew that, he had no idea, but he knew. A Mexican man named Enrique Gonzales—a man in his fifties—snored loudly, cuddling an empty bottle of whiskey. His wife, Rosa, was in her early twenties. As she cooked him breakfast, she yelled at him to get out of bed.

"If water were wine, you'd be taking a bath in it right now! Get up!"

Enrique snorted; he could hear her yelling, but he couldn't care less. He rolled over and went back to sleep.

"That's it! I'm leaving!"

Randy tried to talk to the sleeping, drunken man. "Wow, buddy, better do what she says—get up dude. She's hot. You don't want to lose this chick."

But the man didn't budge. Rosa walked right through Randy, bringing her husband's breakfast to the bedroom. He continued to snore. She began swearing at him, and then threw the food—and the plate—on his face. As she cried hysterically, she packed her bags and then left. As she walked down the road, she lamented.

"Why didn't I listen to my father? I left my home for this? God help me!"

She was statuesque and considered to be the most desirable woman in the land. Though she was quick-minded, she finally gave in to marrying him, after Enrique's lengthy courting and a series of flat-out begging sessions from him. She always knew she had made a terrible mistake; she knew she was better than him, and even her parents pleaded with her not to marry him. But Enrique wouldn't take no for an answer, and he was very persuasive; it didn't matter that he was an outlaw and a professional gambler. As soon as they married—out of the Catholic Church, at a small waterfall followed by a party with his drinking friends—he had her under his thumb, and she couldn't breathe. She had nowhere to go; her father told her never to return if she married Enrique, and her mother pretended she was dead. Only the nunnery would take her in. She retained nothing, including her dignity, so she headed to the nunnery to redeem herself.

A group of Indian ranch hands watched her from a hut. One Indian looked at her with tired and sympathetic eyes.

"What are you looking at, you stupid, dirty Indian?"

The humbled woman looked down with shame as Rosa stomped off.

Randy continued to toss and turn as he dreamed in greater detail.

A handsome Mexican man, Julio Martinez, was hauling a grizzly bear up the road. He had dark hair, big brown eyes, and a thin mustache that neatly lined the top of his lip. His sense of humor could entertain a dozen kings. He passed her slowly, sitting proudly atop his horse. He stared at her seductively, and she stopped as they shared a moment. The bear growled, and Rosa screamed. Then she stomped her foot into the ground and yelled at Julio.

"What are you looking at?" She walked away, down the path and out of sight.

Still half-asleep, Enrique noticed pieces of food on his lips. He licked the egg off with his large, dry tongue.

"Delicious eggs…"

He licked his lips like a dog licking a bowl clean, but as soon as he opened his eyes, he realized the food was all over his face. Then he remembered hearing Rosa yell. He jumped out of bed and ran down the dusty road after her.

"Rosa! Rosa! Come back! I'll never drink again, I promise!"

But Rosa had disappeared. The Indians watched Enrique, trying not to laugh.

"You think this is funny, you bastard Indians? My servants dare to laugh at me?"

He stumbled over to them and backhanded one of them to the ground. The Indian's wife screamed, running to her husband. Enrique kicked her in the face as she lay on the ground, holding her husband.

"Goddamn Indians! You are all cursed! It's all your fault!"

Julio rode up to Enrique, pulling the grizzly bear in the wooden cart. The bear growled fiercely.

"Julio, my man! You have a bear for me?" Enrique looked closely at the bear. The bear growled even louder.

"Careful! He wasn't very happy when he woke up stuck in the cage."

Enrique looked into the bear's eyes. The bear let out the loudest roar yet, which made Enrique nervous. He was desperately hungover and swampy in the head. But he knew what would fix that.

"Perfect! Perfect! Come; let's drink!"

Julio jumped off of the horse, and the two men embraced, pounding each other roughly on the back. They left the bear and the Indians and walked back to the house. Julio looked back at the Indians.

"What's going on around here? Your hair—it has pieces of— what is that stuff?" he asked as he reached for the bits of scrambled eggs stuck in his "macho" friend's thick hair.

"Oh, yeah," replied Enrique, once again recalling how his Rosa stomped out.

Meanwhile, the Indians stared at the noisy and burdened beast. They joined hands in a circle around the cage and began to sing the "bear song." The bear fell to his knees and then fell asleep.

As the two men drank, a small man in a horse and carriage pulled up with his wife and his fourteen kids. He stopped the horse, telling the family to stay put. His wife pulled one of her tiny, curious children back into the covered area of the carriage. Poncho Lopez walked to the front of the house, dropped to his knees, and knocked on the heavy, wooden door.

"Sorry; I am only into women," a drunken and sarcastic Julio said, looking down at the man on his knees and starting to laugh.

As Poncho lowered his head, Enrique swung the door wide open and chuckled. Julio, in his perverse mentality, looked at him and exclaimed, "Enrique, why didn't you tell me you're a man-lover?"

Enrique grunted and threw Poncho across the room.

"A violent man-lover!" Julio exclaimed.

"Please, please, my family is out there," Poncho said, begging for mercy.

"I want my money," Enrique said.

"It's not that I don't have it," Poncho stuttered. "I just don't have it right here, right now."

Enrique picked him up and backhanded him, sending him flying, once again, across the floor. He was bleeding from his mouth.

"Can't you give him some pigs? Chickens? A sheep?" Julio asked, but Enrique's rage boiled.

"He's got nothing! Nothing but fourteen kids and a wife!"

A small pregnant woman with tears in her eyes appeared at the door.

"Looks like fifteen—there's another one on the way!" Julio shouted.

The woman slowly walked through the room, past her beaten husband and over to the last standing table in the room. She took off a gold chain with a cross on it and laid it on the table.

Her husband cried, "No!"

Then she removed her wedding ring and laid it on the table next to the chain.

Poncho screamed, "No, mamacita! No!"

She glanced at her bleeding husband as tears welled up in his eyes. Then she blurted out the word "Puropedo" and walked out. Enrique picked up the items and held them up in the light. He nodded his head in approval of the payment.

Julio peeked out of another window in the front. Poncho's wife was driving the horse and wagon away, with all of the kids.

"Hey!" he yelled out. "You forgot your husband!"

Julio and Enrique stood over Poncho.

"I think he needs a drink," Enrique said.

Poncho popped his head up in agreement.

"And a new wife," Julio added. Poncho dropped his head and began sobbing.

That night, the men hosted a big fiesta. Poncho was still there, passed out in a drunken stupor. Julio looked upon the attractive women who served food and drinks. During the feast, two grizzly bears remained in separate cages. Enrique got up to make a toast to his friend, Julio, who brought him his bear. "To my friend, my compadre, the only man I know who is braver than the all-mighty grizzly himself, Julio Gonzales!"

Everyone cheered and drank. When they emptied the bottles, they simply threw them on the floor, where they shattered. They liked the sound, which made for more festivities. Julio sat with two gorgeous ladies, one on each side. He stood up to lift his glass for the toast, but he missed it.

"Oh, well," he thought.

As he guzzled the rest of the alcohol in his glass, one of the ladies pulled him in closer. She wanted him all to herself. The other one became jealous and grabbed him, which resulted in an argument. Julio ignored the commotion, instead staring at Rosa, who stood on the other side of the room. Her long, black hair and smooth skin glowing in the moonlight transfixed him. He pulled himself away from the two women and walked over to Rosa.

"Why were you in such a hurry this morning?"

"I'm sorry; have we met?" Rosa asked, knowing exactly who he was.

"Do I look like an idiot to you?" Julio responded to her game.

"Maybe I don't like the stench of bear."

"But you do like the smell of love and power, don't you?" Julio said, moving in closer.

"Who doesn't?" Rosa asked, with a fervent grin as she pulled a small jar of alcohol from her bosom and took a swig.

Through blurred vision and a bit of dizziness, she scanned the room for her violent-tempered husband.

"My name is Rosa, wife of Enrique." She offered her hand, and he bent down on one knee and kissed it.

"Rosa, my favorite flower. Tell me, why would something as precious as a rose be drinking like that?"

Just then, a completely intoxicated Enrique stumbled over.

"I see you have met my wife." He slapped her hard across the face. "You leave me again, and I will kill you."

He grabbed Julio's arm, strongly escorting him away.

"It's time for the fight!" Enrique yelled.

The crowd began passing a large burlap bag. One man collected gambling money, while the other stuffed the money in the bag. The men yelled for the fight to start.

Ramon Rodriguez, the contender who brought the other bear to fight, approached Enrique.

"Prepare to lose, my friend."

The comment didn't faze Enrique.

"I have lost my last fight to you. Enjoy your drink, Ramon. Your drunkenness is as good as it's going to get tonight. I will lose to no one."

The men released the bears from the cages, but they left them tied up. The animals were hungry, tired, and outraged. They began to fight. The men shouted for their chosen bear.

As the bears began to rip into each other, the ranch-hand Indians danced around a fire. As the drums got louder and louder, people continued to cheer on the bloody confrontation. Ramon's bear went down.

Enrique's bear turned around and looked Enrique in the eye. Never so intensely had an animal looked at a man. The bear sensed it was Enrique who had organized the fight.

Enrique laughed as Ramon fell to his knees and placed his head on the ground. He had bet everything he owned on this fight. He needed it to save his ranch.

"Of course I won! And you lose! You lose! You lose!"

Enrique cared about one thing and one thing only: himself. Then Enrique's bear tried to charge at him, but it could not break away from the restraints. With a vengeance, he tried and tried again. Enrique searched frantically for his gun, but he couldn't find it.

The Indians powerfully danced around the fire, giving strength to the beast. A wild screech—not human, not animal, but something supernatural—came from the nearby bushes. The face of Pogonip, the river ghost, appeared. His eyes glowed red, and his long, black hair flew in the wind, as if every strand took on a life of its own. Then, as suddenly as he appeared, the fog devoured him.

At that moment, the bear broke free and attacked Enrique. No one tried to save him. The last thing Enrique saw before he died was Rosa licking the barrel of his gun, ever so slowly, like an ice cream cone. She smiled and waved good-bye to him.

"Are you ready to go?" Julio asked gallantly.

"I was born ready," Rosa replied.

Taking advantage of the confusion, Rosa grabbed the burlap bag of money collected from the fight and jumped on Julio's horse. As they rode down the dark, dirt road, the horse slowed near the

Indians' fire. Rosa ordered Julio to stop. She jumped off of the horse and walked up to the Indians.

"I am sorry. I am truly sorry for all of the pain I have caused you. I never meant to cause any of you grief. I have been a very unhappy woman. Now I am free. Please find it in your hearts to forgive me."

Tears flowed down her face. The Indian woman whom Enrique had beaten earlier embraced Rosa. Rosa felt like a sister to her because they had shared the same perpetrator. The Indian woman recognized this and forgave Rosa. As she pulled away, she kissed her forehead.

"Go. Go while you still can."

And with that, a gunshot went off in the near distance, and the women heard the cry of a wounded bear. The horse got spooked, and Julio dragged Rosa onto the horse's back as it began to run. When the horse slowed to a calmer pace, Rosa questioned Julio.

"Why didn't you tell me you were Chinese?"

"What? Who said I was Chinese?"

Randy woke up to the sound of the bloodcurdling scream from Pogonip as the soul of the great grizzly was set free and its longtime tormentor, Enrique, died.

Randy was lying in a pool of sweat. His window was wide open, and the white curtains flew wildly. When he got up to close them, he saw the back of a horse riding off with a man and a woman, with long black hair flying behind her. He knew that never happened on his street, and he also knew he wasn't seeing things. Everything was getting weirder and weirder.

His mind started to race.

"Why did Rosa say Julio was Chinese after all of that? And why are my legs sore?"

Then he remembered the beginning of the dream. Dennis, the Indian guy, was in it. He wondered whether Dennis could get into his dreams, just like he did his mind.

TWENTY-ONE

Randy and Eric stood in front of the school, while a faceless mass of kids swarmed by, but when Leslie walked up, Eric focused all his attention. "Hey, uh…"

"I know you can put a sentence together because I heard you do it before," Leslie said, giving him a flirtatious look.

Randy butted in: "Oh, yeah? Well, we found a foot yesterday!"

"Excuse me?" said Leslie.

Eric took her arm, saying, "Let me walk you to class."

"You guys are sick; you know that?" Thomas said, walking in on the conversation. "Sick!"

Randy chuckled. "What can I say? It really happened! Did your dad come home?"

"No," Thomas said. "The police called my mom this morning. I don't know what happened yet."

"Dude. I'm sorry, man."

As Holly Hartford walked by, Randy couldn't help but hit on her.

"Oh, yeah, baby; how would you like a big, red-hot chili pepper or a big beefy burrito?"

Holly was disgusted.

"You're not flattering me in the least. In fact, you're grossing me out."

Viper swooped in out of nowhere.

"She doesn't eat Mexican food. She only eats filet mignon. Tube steak, if you will. So why don't you take your little chili pepper and shove it where the sun doesn't shine?"

"You're right; you're right. I'm wrong," Randy said as he moved closer to hug Viper.

But instead, he threw him to the ground. Viper immediately stood up, acting like nothing had happened; he didn't want any more trouble at school.

"I'm not taking the wrap for this," he yelled as he ran off.

Tim rushed over, but Viper was gone.

"What just happened here?" Tim demanded.

"I don't know, but is that a cha cha cha chia pet growing on your head? Cha cha cha chia—remember that one?" Randy taunted him, laughing.

"You're a smart ass now and you're going to smart ass your way to jail," Tim said, trying to cover up his hurt feelings.

Then he got up in Randy's face.

"You know how they take it in prison? Straight up and all the way in. You like chocolate, don't you?"

Tim cringed at the thought, as if it very well may have happened to him. He paused for a moment, looking off in the distance and beginning to quiver uncontrollably. Randy was horrified, and Thomas couldn't believe his ears.

"Okay, man, you are trippin', and I have to be somewhere," Thomas said, walking away from Tim.

"I don't know how much more I can take this week." Randy followed Thomas, looking back and thinking about how the school hired such a nasty man to protect students. It was just more proof that the world was upside down, and there wasn't much hope for any goodness at all.

But Tim wasn't really a nasty man. He just wanted to scare them a little. He was so far out of his league; he had no idea what the hell he was doing. He began to think he would have been much better off at a gardening shop or something.

Inside, the class settled down as Randy came in late. Ms. Rowanna was speaking to the class.

"I don't know where he is…" she said. Randy thought she was talking about him.

"I'm here. I am sorry I am late," Randy said.

As he looked for his chair, he passed Leslie, who was sitting next to Eric in the front row.

"I wasn't talking about you, Randy," Ms. Rowanna said. "But would you please sit next to Howard today? We have another speaker—I hope he is coming."

Randy had no intention of sitting next to Howard.

"I don't think that's such a good idea," Randy said.

"What did you say?" Rowanna asked in a stern voice.

"I'm not sitting next to him."

"Why is that?"

Just then the guest speaker, Jim Lee, walked in. He was an athletic Chinese man in his late fifties.

"Oh, good. You're here," Rowanna said. "Class: This is Jim Lee. He grew up here in Chinatown. Jim, how are you?"

She gave him a warm handshake and a pat on the back.

"Good, good. Sorry I'm late. The traffic is backed up on Mission Street."

"Oh, you came up Mission Street? I know how that is."

Randy was still standing in the middle of the class. Jim looked over at him.

"I see the gang is all here."

"Would you please sit down, young man?" Rowanna said, her voice on edge.

Randy reluctantly sat down next to Howard. Howard turned to look at him, in what seemed like slow motion to Randy. His face appeared bloodied and bruised. It pissed off Randy to look at

Howard's pitiful face after he had beaten it in the other day, but he also felt a little twinge of remorse. Mr. Lee looked at Howard's face.

"What happened to you? Get hit by a bus?"

"I uh, I uh—nothing," Howard said, stuttering.

Jim knew Howard's father well.

"He got beat up," Randy said, as he put his arm around Howard. "Don't worry, Mr. Lee; I'll look after him from now on."

"I am going to hold you to your word, young man," Jim said sternly. "We are like family."

Jim moved in close to Randy and whispered to him, "The Chinese Martial Arts has the widest array of weapons of any ancient culture ever known to man, and I know how to use every one of them. Have I made myself clear?"

Randy drew an instant sweat and swallowed hard.

"Yes, sir," said Randy.

The Chinese community was very small and close-knit in Santa Cruz. Everyone knew everyone, and people didn't keep secrets—or withhold names of bullies—among those in their circle.

TWENTY-TWO

Jim Lee began to tell the class the story of Chinatown. "It was 1864..." Once again, a vortex pulled the students and Rowanna right into the story. "There was a huge explosion. Twelve Chinese workers were terrified and covered from head to toe in white powder. They ran for their lives out of the factory. A couple of white guys stood there in disbelief, watching the factory smoke and cheering on the Chinese men as they stopped just outside the factory to catch their breath.

"When the Civil War cut off California's supply of explosives, which was vital to all types of construction, the California Powder Works was established. It was located on the San Lorenzo River, a mile up from Santa Cruz. A dozen Chinese laborers arrived at the powder factory. They were the first sizable group of Chinese in the Santa Cruz area, and they established Chinatown.

"At that time, Chinatown consisted of a temple, a couple of stores, and a row of laundries. They built thin and tall wooden structures. Inside the laundry facilities, dozens of ironing boards lined the walls. A dozen men washed the clothes and bedding in washtubs, located at the rear of the room. After they pounded the water out of the linens and clothing, they hung them on lines outside the building. They ironed by hand, with irons heated on a charcoal stove. Whenever an iron cooled, they traded it for a hot one. Off-duty men slept under ironing boards, ready for their shift when it came around.

"Only one store catered to whites. This is where the Chinese rolled several thousand cigars each week, in full view of passersby. Pieces of dried fruit and specialty food hung around the store.

"Initially, most of the Chinese people came to California because of revolt, war, and economic difficulty. The California Gold Rush offered an opportunity for a better life. The geographical and climatic similarities between California and their homeland made it easy for the Chinese to adapt to the farming and fishing trade in the U.S.

"But once again, as fate would have it, nothing would be easy for the Chinese in Santa Cruz. This Chinatown, like the ones to follow, provided refuge only to those who washed dishes, cooked, did laundry, made beds, and waited on tables.

"Meanwhile, a group of Yankees tried to turn Santa Cruz into the image of New England. They built limekilns, tanneries, and lumber mills everywhere; they capitalized on Santa Cruz's natural resources, especially the San Lorenzo River, which offered both water and power. At one point, Santa Cruz had a higher population of whites than anywhere else in the state. Most of them employed a Chinese houseboy or cook. If it weren't for the Chinese, there would be no railroads. No one else was willing to do the work because it was pure torture."

TWENTY-THREE

"One day," Jim Lee continued his story, "an old man was slaving away, building the railroad tracks. His face was mutilated from a past not so fortunate. Sweat dripped off his neck as the blistering heat penetrated his sore back like a thousand bee stings. After an entire lifetime of working in the same position, he developed a hunchback and had to rise up slowly just to wipe his neck and take a look around.

"He remembered a time many years ago when he did the same work, only he was in love. The heavy labor didn't matter; love changed everything for him. He lived in a dream of the past, but it was the only thing he had to live for. And it was better than nothing at all.

"He remembered one Chinese New Year, so long ago. A spectacular parade of people marched down the street. Firecrackers and fireworks lit up the night sky. Bright and colorful lamps hung off balconies and overhangs. Dandies and goodies were being handed out to everyone, including the white people who watched from the sidewalks. The old man—back in the days when he was much younger—demonstrated a martial arts form. He was daring, handsome, and full of hope. He thought nothing could stop him or bring him down.

"That night, he met Jezebel—oh, sweet Jezebel. Everything softened when he thought of her and the memories they once shared."

As Jim Lee talked about the two lovers, Eric gazed at Leslie. But Leslie was completely absorbed with Jim Lee's story.

"Jezebel was there with her best friend, Betsy. The biggest mistake of his life—and the best thing that ever happened to him—was seeing Jezebel that night. But the truth is, he didn't see her first; she noticed him and followed him down the street as he moved along with the parade.

"'Who is that?' Jezebel asked Betsy, gesturing to the man.

"'How am I supposed to know? Jezebel, where are you going?'

"'I just want to get a better look at him,' Jezebel said. 'Are you coming?'

"Without waiting for her friend's reply, she pushed through the crowds as discreetly as she could to keep up with him. He finally caught her eye, nearly immobilizing her.

"Later that night, Jezebel dreamed of the moment she laid eyes on the future love of her life. But then, she heard a loud screeching—not human, not animal—like nothing she had ever heard before. Drums began to play, louder and louder, and it looked as if some kind of a demon was coming at her. He had long black hair, which flew wildly, like the wind. She could see his face; he was an Indian. Within moments, he faded as quickly as he had appeared.

"She woke up earlier than usual the next morning, remembering the dream; it seemed so real it startled her to the point of taking her breath away. Feeling groggy and confused, she pulled herself out of bed and walked downstairs. She smelled bacon on the grill and heard the sound of her family cheerfully laughing. It made her feel safe to think about her strong father who always protected her and her smart, loving mother who guided her through difficulties. Most of her friends didn't like their own little brothers, but she loved little Thomas with all of her heart."

TWENTY-FOUR

"Jezebel's mother," continued Jim Lee, "worked around the table, where everyone was properly seated. Jezebel's white-bred father always pushed his opinions on everyone.

"'Them China boys really know how to put on a show!' he said.

"'Father, why do you call them China boys? Most of them are old men,' Jezebel said.

"Her father chuckled, as his big belly bounced up and down. 'Who you callin' old? Maybe if they were bigger than three feet tall, I could call 'em something else, but fer now, it's China boys.'

"'Maybe they aren't so short after all,' she said, defiantly.

"Her mother turned around from the stove as the bacon grease sizzled. Everyone listened in on Jezebel, who wasn't normally so argumentative.

"'Maybe they just seem smaller because they are always bending over doing someone else's dirty work.'

"Jezebel's mother threw the dishtowel over her shoulder and leaned over the sink to rinse her face with water and said, 'Oh Lord have mercy above! My daughter is sticking up for the celestials!'

"'I will not have no heathen, devil Chinese lovin' daughter in my house!' her father said, pounding his fist on the table while Thomas hid his face in his hands. 'Those bastard rats are takin' up our jobs! They be thinkin' they can just come over here and take our gold and take all of our jobs and use up all of our land—well, they got another thing comin'! They be good fer nothin'! You hear? Nothin!'

"Everyone sat around the table, silent.

"Later that afternoon, Jezebel walked through Chinatown, shopping for fruit. She carried a huge basket. She approached a peddler who had packed produce into two baskets he balanced on shoulder poles. His produce measured three times the size of normal vegetables and fruit. She filled up her basket and quickly moved on, making sure to keep to herself. But then she bumped into the martial artist from the parade the night before. They both tried to say something, but an uncomfortable silence pervaded. The Chinese and the whites did not mix on a social level back then—especially a young Chinese man and a young white woman.

"A bit embarrassed, Jezebel walked backwards in an attempt to soak in every unspoken moment with him—it was a moment unlike any she had ever felt; the world stood still, and she didn't have a care in the world when she looked into his eyes. The sky looked bluer. Everything smelled good, and nothing could alter her mood.

"When she arrived home, Jezebel sat with her mother at the kitchen table. She smelled the flowers while she arranged a bouquet of mostly roses, which her mother had picked from the garden.

"'Oh, mother, this rose smells sweeter than any other rose I have smelled before!'

"Her mother recognized her 'mood.'

"'Who is he?'

"Jezebel giggled.

"'Why mother! You couldn't possibly think…you know…'

"'I don't think anything. I know. I am your mother. Remember? Mothers know everything there is to know—now tell me everything.'

"Jezebel hesitated as her mother went on.

"'You are eighteen now. I have been waiting for this for a long time, Jessie. Please don't treat me like a stranger; you know how much I love you.'

"'Mother, do you believe in love at first sight?'

"Looking off into the distance for a moment, her mother became lost in her own story.

"'Well, yes, I do. But who is it that you haven't seen before? No one new has moved into town, or have they?'

"'Not exactly, Mother.'

"Meanwhile, in a Chinatown home, the martial artist gazed at himself in a tiny mirror. He was strikingly handsome. He had high cheekbones and large brown eyes. His teeth were bright white and very straight. His thick hair framed his face in a carefree manner. He had practiced his English. The pronunciations were so different than his native language; he struggled to curl the words correctly, especially around the letters L and R. He practiced with different tones and moods, just in case he might need them some day. But right now, he tried to be sincere.

"'Hi. My na is Lam … Her-o, my na is Lam.'

"Lam wiped his forehead, trying harder.

"'Heyo, my na is Lam.'

"What was the use of trying to talk to Jezebel if he couldn't speak right? He tried for a romantic tone.

"'Heyo. My na is Lam.'

"It was his best attempt, and he intended to get the most use out of it.

"When he met Jezebel and Betsy again, he whispered in a humble manner, as he lowered his head out of respect for Jezebel.

"'Hello. My name is Lam.'

"Delighted, Jezebel replied, 'I am Jezebel Emily Riley Sternbigenber Rosellmeyer. It's really Jezebel Emily Riley Sternbigenber Rosellmeyer III,' Jezebel added, stumbling on her words. 'But don't tell anyone that because that kind of identification is only suited for the gentleman kind. Oh, and this is my best friend, Betsy.'

"Lam tried to keep up with the ladies' dialogue, but they had lost him. He nodded his head, smiling, as if he understood every word they said.

"'You know: The first, the second, the third; it's just that the name Jezebel Emily Riley Sternbigenber has been on my mother's side for three generations now, and when she met my father, well, you can imagine, and of course, she had to add his name on there—Rosellmeyer....'

"She was so giddy she could hardly contain herself. Betsy looked at her like she had lost her mind. Jezebel shrugged her shoulders and continued to giggle.

"'She doesn't get out much,' Betsy said, trying to cut the absurd tension. 'We usually keep her locked up in the barn.'

"'Oh no!' Lam exclaimed, not getting the joke.

"Jezebel gasped and nudged Betsy's arm, feeling embarrassed.

"'Betsy! We really must be getting on our way now.'

"They scurried off, skipping and laughing. Betsy turned around and yelled, 'We feed her through a little crack in the barn!'

"Lam laughed a bit and shook his head in agreement, as if he knew they were joking, but inside, he hoped Jezebel didn't really live in a barn.

"Not long after, Jezebel's father and a few of his buddies sat at Wong Kee's gambling parlor and opium den, located above Wong Kee's only brick-front store in Chinatown. The store sold everything the Chinese community needed, including dried seaweed, fried shark fins, eggs from China, candles, nuts, and fruit. Behind the cash register sat a photo of Wong's deceased wife, with a candle burning in front of it. The gambling parlor was upstairs, and it employed two beautiful prostitutes. Jezebel's father eyed one of the girls.

"Lam showed up while Wong was out running some errands. He overheard the men treating the girls poorly: Jezebel's father hit one of them and knocked over some bottles. Lam ran upstairs to find him raping one of the girls while the others watched. Lam tried to tear Jezebel's father away from her, but the onlookers jumped him and beat him.

"The next morning, the sun shone intensely upon the San Lorenzo River. Jezebel sat by the water's edge and threw a pebble in. Immediately, someone behind a bush threw in another pebble. She did it again, and another pebble flew out from the bush into the river. She smiled and ran over to the bush. It was Lam.

"They had to meet in secret, or her father would punish her and separate them for good. They hadn't yet touched, but a mutual love and respect had developed.

"'Lam! What's wrong? Why won't you come out of the bushes?' Jezebel asked him.

"Lam moved toward her, keeping his head down, lowered and hidden. Jezebel dropped to her knees and reached up to his face. 'What happened?'

"His face was completely swollen. He had two black eyes and a broken nose. She hardly recognized him. She gasped in horror and held her hands over her mouth, as tears rolled down his face. The salt burned the open cuts. He couldn't utter a word, or he would break down completely.

"She put his face in her hands and kissed his wet, salty cheeks for the very first time. Her lips finally met his and they embraced. She held him like a baby as he sobbed in her loving arms for over an hour until the sadness subsided.

"Over the course of the time they spent together, Lam told her all about what it was like living in his homeland, China. He also explained how the Chinese language used symbols. Chinese words looked like art to her, and the sound of his voice was like no music she had ever heard.

"She, in return, told him about her childhood years and how much fun she had growing up in Santa Cruz. She taught him how to pronounce English better and how to act like an American. But Lam didn't respond as quickly as she had hoped.

"Afterward, she ran into her house, screaming at her father. At first, he thought someone had hurt her. He grabbed her to comfort her, but she kicked and slapped him. He backhanded her, and she fell to the ground. Her mouth bled. Her mother watched from a safe distance, and Thomas hid in a nearby bush.

"'It's that rat-eating, law-ignorin' China boy that Betsy told me about, isn't it?'

"Jezebel couldn't believe it: Betsy promised never to say a word.

"'That's right. Can't no one keep a secret 'round here! Pretty soon the whole town's gonna know!' He paced around her like an angry wolf. 'What you thinkin' girl? You gonna marry a half-human, Christian civilization hater?'

"He kicked her in the ribs as his anger grew. 'If I didn't know any better, I wouldn't be sure if I was looking at Satan himself right now,' he said, kicking her a few more times.

"Her mother ran out crying and threw her body over her daughter's to protect her.

"'Stop it! Stop it! You are killing her!'

"Tears poured from Jezebel's eyes, down her soft, innocent face, as she shook uncontrollably.

"'I love him, Mommy. You know what it means to be in love. He works hard. He cares for me and loves me too. Love doesn't mean the color of someone's skin. I know that for sure because it happened to me. Please don't hate me, Mommy. I love you so much. What you think about me means everything. Please don't hate me.'

"Thomas stuck his thumb in his mouth and ran out from the bush to sit in the dirt next to them. Jezebel's father cursed God and stomped into the house. He screamed like a crazy monster, throwing dishes in the kitchen. Jezebel's mother huddled in the dirt with her children until he finally stormed out of the house and left.

"That cold, foggy afternoon changed everything. Indian drumming wafted through the air as Jezebel's mouth bled. Her father had broken her jaw and knocked out a few of her teeth. She held her broken ribcage as she walked over to the Santa Cruz cliffs and climbed down a big rock to the water's edge. The drumming intensified; she could hear it—it was the same drumming she had heard in her dream. She cried out hysterically. Betsy could hear her through the fog.

"'Jezebel! Jezebel!' Betsy finally found her. 'What are you doing? Wait for me!'

"Betsy feared she would jump. She stopped at the edge of the cliff and looked down at her friend. The drumming became louder and louder, and then the girls heard a loud scream, not human, not animal. She could hear Jezebel wailing.

"'Jezebel!' She climbed down to sit with her. 'Jesse, what happened to you? What happened to us? I want my best friend back.' She tried to hug her, but Jezebel pulled away. 'Remember when we used to climb old Mrs. Whimble's cypress tree to look into Jed Barker's bedroom? Oh, Lordy! If anyone found out about that! If only the whole world could see freckle-faced Jed Baker dancing around in his underclothes like that! What was he thinking?' Betsy giggled, trying to cheer up her friend.

"Jezebel stopped crying and looked into the water, expressionless.

"'How about that time your mama got real sick and we thought she was going to die and we stayed up all night singing prayers to the good Lord up above, and then that big white light came and filled up the room and it got real warm as if Jesus himself were there to pay us a visit,' Betsy said, hoping to get through to her friend. 'Then she woke up the next morning and was walking around with that grin on her face like nothing ever happened.'

"Jezebel fell into a trance, glaring into the foamy ocean water. The drumming started up again.

"Dusk had settled in on Chinatown, along with a thick fog. Jezebel's father had organized a candlelight parade to march through Chinatown, and nearly one hundred people showed up. The group chanted: 'Chinese go home!'

"On the cliffs, Jezebel finally spoke. 'My heart is weak. I have nothing now. The world isn't what I thought it was. Why did I ever trust you?'

"'I was doing the best I could for you,' Betsy said. 'You could never marry a mongrel!'

"'How could you possibly know what's best for me? You're not even human.'

"'You're the devil!' Betsy said, pulling herself off the shoreline. 'You are not my friend! That is it. Never again! I wish I never met you! I hate you!'

"Back in town, various people cursed at the Chinese as they paraded from house to house. They covered their faces and heads in dark cloth disguises. A baby boy and his sister peeked out of a window, watching in horror as a group carried candles and chanted: 'Death to the Chinese. Death to the Chinese...'

"As Betsy climbed up the rocks to get away, she lost her balance. Jezebel caught her, saving her from the fall, only to fall herself into a thunderous wave. As the drums roared, the non-animal, non-human Pogonip ghost collected his victim and let out a blood-curdling howl.

"'Jezebel! Jezebel! Jezebel!'

"Jezebel grabbed a rock and almost made it out of the water, but another wave slammed her into the jagged rocks. As her hand reached toward another rock, her fingers slid away, into the foggy foam of the great Pacific Ocean.

"After Jezebel's death, Lam was heartbroken. White people continuously beat him for months and months. With his background in martial arts, he could have fought back and won. But he knew, ultimately, he didn't stand a chance with the war on racism. Nor did he care. The world seemed upside down; nothing mattered to him anymore. He surrendered himself to working on the railroad for the rest of his life.

"Yes, he remembered a time when life was worth living: When he was young and in love with Jezebel. He stood back up for a moment as a tear rolled down his face.

"Not much changed for the Chinese for twenty-five years or so. It was nearly the turn-of-the century, and despite their hard work, the Chinese remained predominately dominated by the white man."

As Jim finished the story of Chinatown, the classroom remained quiet. Even Randy felt sad. As soon as the bell rang, he ran out as fast as he could. He revved up his monster truck and burned rubber out of the school parking lot. He drove out to the cliffs and parked, then hiked down a cliff.

"NOOOOOOOO!"

Randy screamed at the wind and broke down. Eric had followed him and pulled up as his friend cried.

"I'm not Mexican, man," Randy said through his sobbing tears. "My real mother was Chinese. She died. She died having me! I hate myself!"

He stood up and yelled at the top of his lungs.

"I hate myself!"

He fell to the ground.

"Please help me."

Tears welled up in Eric's eyes as he put his arm around Randy. Both boys felt so small on the cliffs, with the vast ocean in front of them.

"I wouldn't care if you were from outer space. You're my bro, and nothing can come between us."

Randy whimpered. Then he calmed down and stared out at the water.

"You promise?" Randy said, his voice hoarse.

"Of course I promise. But do you think you could be a little nicer to other people now? Poor Howard. You really did a number on him."

Randy thought about it in silence, until they both started to laugh. Having to say such a thing was so absurd—even they knew it. Randy wiped his eyes with his shirt.

"I'm starving. I could really go for some stir-fry and spring rolls." It was the first time in a long while that Randy admitted he missed his family's signature meal.

TWENTY-FIVE

The next day, thunderous clouds rolled in. Holly's hair was sopping wet, and she was late to class. When she ran into the school, she felt like someone was watching her, but she didn't notice anyone right away. Then she turned and saw Tim staring at her. He was leaning up against the trophy display. A bolt of lightning struck, and she let out a scream.

"You know, you almost scared me half to death," she said to him, flipping her long blond hair over her shoulder.

"Class is in session," Tim said. "Better run along now."

"No," Holly replied. "I am already late, so it doesn't really matter. I know it's none of my business, but I have to say this: I don't think you are such a bald guy—I mean 'bad guy.' I don't know why I even care. But I really think if you lost the rug on your head, you could probably get a date. I mean, I don't know what your head looks like, but you have a cute face, for an old guy. Most guys who are losing their hair shave it off so you can't tell. Bald—or almost bald—is in. But then there's the matter of your clothes. Wear black. Black pants, a black short-sleeve T-shirt—not too baggy—in fact, snug fitting is best, and a black casual sports jacket. I'm telling you, it'll change your world. I don't know why I am telling you all of this, or how I even thought of it. There's just something about you."

As she walked toward room number nine, she turned around to say one last thing to him.

"Oh, yeah, and stop trying so hard to be normal. You are normal. You don't have to fake it to fit in. It's really annoying. Just be yourself."

She had felt sorry for Tim since the first minute she laid eyes on him. She sensed that deep down inside, he really was a nice guy—a nice guy who was just trying to reinvent his life. But she wondered where all of her concern and suggestions came from. She handed a tardy slip to her teacher and took a seat in the classroom.

Tim stood in the hallway, dumfounded by Holly's comments.

"Was that out of left field or what?" he thought. He wondered if he took her advice, could he find someone who would love him—or even look at him? Then again, what was he thinking listening to Holly? What if she was trying to trick him into something? But then again, she was an attractive senior ready to graduate into adulthood in less than a year. Surely she knew what she was talking about. Maybe he would think about it—maybe. He pulled out his trusty notebook and jotted down everything she told him to do—just in case.

TWENTY-SIX

"I hope the class is enjoying this semester as much as I am," Ms. Rowanna said to the class. Lightning struck and lit up her face. "We have so much to learn and so little time—wouldn't you say? Who would like to start our discussion today?"

Holly raised her hand. "I can't believe how awful we were to the Chinese. I mean, we just flat out dragged them through the coals. Why did it have to be like that?"

"If I could answer that question, I would," said Ms. Rowanna. "Now let me ask you one: Why is knowing our history important?" The class remained silent. "Does anybody get it?"

She waited, but she could tell that none of her students knew what to say.

"Why is it okay to treat each other poorly now, but not okay for people who did it in the past? Looking back, we can clearly see that we were wrong. What right do we have to judge them, or anyone for that matter—ever? Haven't we all put down people, at one time or another?"

Still nothing, but she trusted she had the students thinking—she didn't notice any dead eyes. She could tell they were all scrambling around for answers in their minds, trying to find their place within it all.

"Because from an outsider's perspective, things look a little different, don't they? So maybe that's why we need to learn from history." Ms. Rowanna walked slowly around the room. "Because life repeats itself, over and over again. And by looking at other people's mistakes, maybe..."

She paused and looked at Randy. "Just maybe we can learn from them."

Then she looked at Holly.

"And maybe we can change. Don't ever listen to anyone who tells you that you can't change."

She tapped her pudgy finger on Randy's desk.

"Change yourself for the better and *you will change the world for the better.*"

Randy looked meekly at Howard and gave him a crooked half-smile. Eric raised his hand.

"I brought some photos of my great-grandfather, Fred Swanson."

"Why don't you stand up and tell us about him?" Rowanna said. "Do you mind passing them around?"

"Um, okay. This one is of him and his cousin, Fred Parshly. When they were young, they brought the telephone to Santa Cruz. Well, at least that's what I heard. They were around twenty or twenty-one."

He handed the photo to the teacher first. Eric began to tell the story about what happened as the class drifted back into history once again.

"Fred and Fred were trying out a new telephone line in the house. When it vibrated in the stable, they were elated it worked. My grandpa Swanson answered the call."

Eric launched into the story, telling it as if it were happening again.

"'Hello? Jumpin' jeepers cousin! It works! It works!'

"Parshly spoke on the other end of the line.

"'Can you hear me?'

"'Can I hear you? I can practically smell you!'

"Swanson jumped up and down, shaking his arms and yelling. A Chinese servant walked by with a pile of dirty dishes stacked up in his arms. Swanson grabbed him.

"'Listen! It's a telephone; can you hear, Fred? My cousin, he's all the way out in the stable; can you hear him?'

"Swanson put the phone up to the servant's ear. The servant dropped all of the dishes; he didn't speak much English, but he knew something big was going on. He muttered a couple of words in Chinese into the phone. Swanson picked him up in the air and swung him around.

"'Do you know what this means?'

"Inside the stable, Parshly remained glued to the receiver.

"'Calm down, Fred; you are fading in and out. Are you moving around?'

"Swanson dropped the servant and stood perfectly still.

"'Can you hear me now? Good. I'll tell you what this means. We are in business, my man! Swanson and Parshly, bringing the voices of Santa Cruz together, making a brighter future for all!'

"As Parshly looked up in the sky, he saw his vision come to life.

"The next day, Swanson and Parshly walked into a local store. Mrs. Whaley, a short, snooty lady in her fifties, stood behind the cash register.

"'Morning, Mrs. Whaley,' Swanson said with a circus act grin. She knew he was up to something.

"'Good morning, Mr. Swanson. Can I help you with something?'

"Swanson always did all of the talking. He was the front man, and Parshly was his sidekick.

"'Actually, Mrs. Whaley, why, Mrs. Whaley, did you do something to your hair? You look years younger and you have a glow about you...'

"She smiled and patted her hair.

"'Fred Swanson, you're the only one who noticed. I had it done two weeks ago. Mr. Whaley hasn't been paying much attention these days.'

"'He's going to be mighty proud of you when I'm finished telling you what I've got!'

"She couldn't wait to hear what he had to say—anything was better than the lack of attention her husband showed. As she tuned in, Swanson made his first telephone sale.

"After that, they visited the sheriff's station.

"'Imagine this: A call comes in the night. It's a woman. She is in distress because she is sure someone is outside of her house, looking in her windows and wanting to get in. Her husband is up north digging for gold. Her five kids are nestled up, asleep. Maybe it's an Indian. Maybe it's a murderer. Who knows what or who it is. All she knows is that it's going to get her, kill her and all of her younglings. She panics and rings for you. She calls you, and you show up immediately. And you catch that person, that murderer. I can see it now: *Sheriff Daly, Local Hero* on the front page of *The Sentinel*. You save an entire family and innocent lives. There's a picture of you and the whole family. And her husband comes back with a sack full of gold, all for you, because you saved his family from the perils of evil. Why, I wouldn't be surprised if that kind of attention might lead to an even higher elected position—or who knows what?'

"Sheriff Daly bought into the vision.

"'How and when Fred Swanson? What do I have to sign and how fast can you get it over here?'

"Swanson's selling abilities amazed Parshly. He pulled out a contract, shaking, for the sheriff to sign.

"As they walked home down Pacific Avenue, Parshly was nearly speechless.

"'Who are you?'

"Swanson laughed.

"'I'm your cousin, you blundering fool!'

"Parshly grabbed Swanson abruptly by the arm and stopped him in his tracks, looking him in the eye.

"'Fred, I'm looking at a man I have known all my life. But I feel like I don't know you at all. There's somethin' 'bout you, somethin' different, like you got stars in your eyes, and people can see it.'

"'Why, Parshly, you're looking at the magic of a dreamer, only I'm not sleeping. I'm awake.'"

Eric finished the story with what Fred finished saying: "You'd be amazed what dreamers can do with their eyes wide open."

TWENTY-SEVEN

Eric passed around another picture.

"This one here is of my great-great-grandfather, my great-grandmother, and my great-grandfather after they got married. They had a boarding house called The Swanson House. My great-grandma's name was Emma; she was from Aptos. She was adopted, so we don't really know her bloodline. Anyway, she knew how to play the piano and sing like there was no tomorrow."

Again, Eric began to tell the story of his family as if it were happening as his fellow students listened.

"Inside The Swanson Boarding House, Emma Swanson—Fred's wife, who was in her twenties—played the piano passionately. She was gorgeous and had the best voice in town. Fred's father was A.P. Swanson—short for Albino Paris Swanson. He was a dignified man, hardworking and well into his sixties. They were having a drink with some guests in the parlor.

"Fred said, 'I just don't see why the Chinese must go. They've done nothing but good for the economy.'

"A.P. agreed.

"'They built our railroads...'

"'Look at all they have done for our agriculture and fishing industry,' Fred said, 'and not to mention the Powder Works. They clean our houses, do our laundry, and serve us our food—why, they can do anything and everything!'

"Just then, a Chinese man placed a plate of food on the table.

"'Thank you, Charlie.' A.P. said.

"'See what we mean?' Fred jumped in. 'Who else is going to do it?'

"'I'll tell you who's going to do it,' said Dudley McPierson, a man in his fifties who opposed the Chinese. 'The young white people of our community. And the less privileged. That's who's going to do it.'

"Major Hank T. MacDonald, also in his fifties, who dabbled in everything, including hunting, financing, and Republican politics, agreed.

"'I'll drink to that, Dudley!' They clanked their bottles in a toast.

"MacDonald continued, 'This town has a reputation to hold up, for God sakes; the amended Chinese exclusion Act back in '84 happened for a reason, and that reason was because they are not wanted here.'

"The Major slammed A.P. hard on the back.

"'Now that A.P. here is finally sitting on the Common Council, I'm sure he will be making the right decisions.'

"MacDonald straightened out his jacket and looked around the room. 'Now won't we, partner?'

"A.P. knew once the people elected him to the council, he would have to compromise many things, but he never imagined this. He was a decent man and knew the real meaning of a decision made wrongfully or rightfully.

"Emma returned to the table. 'Can't a girl get any attention around here?' she asked, turning to Fred. 'What do I have to do? Jump up on the table?'

"All of the gentlemen stood up around the table to greet her. She grabbed Fred's drink and guzzled it down.

"Dudley McPierson still fretted over the Chinese.

"'And we started out with six Chinese back in '60! Now there are over five hundred of them,' he said.

"Emma slammed the glass down on the table.

"'Oops! Beg your pardon.'

"She winked at her husband and walked away.

"'Where did you find a woman like that?' McPierson asked with a wink.

"Fred slipped into a daze: He could hear the Pogonip screams. 'Did you hear that?'

"'Son, you have had a long day. Maybe it's time to throw in the towel,' his father said.

"'No, I hear something. Can't you hear it?'

"'No, son.' His father's stern voice shook Fred out of the daze, and he wiped his forehead; he had broken out in a sweat.

"'I must be tired as all heck,' Fred replied. 'After all, I did sell the telephone to all of Santa Cruz today.'"

TWENTY-EIGHT

"Later that night," Eric continued his tale, "MacDonald and McPierson stumbled around the front of the Swanson establishment, waiting for their coaches to arrive. Their voices carried loud and far. McPierson tried to persuade MacDonald to do something.

"'I want you to get it done before you depart for your hunting trip to Africa with Mr. Roosevelt.'

"'Consider it done,' MacDonald said in his usual men's club tone. 'It's already been taken care of.'

"The men were so loud, the local paper reporter, Ernie Odda, couldn't help but overhear them as he walked by.

"'McPierson!'

"The man reached out his hand.

"'Ernie Odda! A future star reporter for *The Sentinel* newspaper. Have you met Major General Hank T. MacDonald?'

"'No, I don't believe I have had the honor; it's very nice to meet you.'

"'Just call me Hank.'

"'Odda, I hear you are going to be working for *The Surf*,' McPierson said.

"The comment caught Odda off-guard; the paper hadn't made it official, and no one was supposed to know yet.

"'Well I, ah…'

"'After all we have done for you, boy, you should be ashamed,' McPierson said. 'What was your first delivery route for? Oh, yes, for my paper, *The Sentinel*, of course!'

"'Actually, it was for *The Courier Item*; then it was for *The Santa Cruz Surf*, *The Daily Sentinel*, *The Daily Echo*, *The Chronicle*, and then *The Examiner*,' replied Odda, feeling he had the upper hand because he was sober.

"Drunk and irritated, McPierson interrupted him. 'Moving on lad; my best to Arthur.'

"McPierson slapped Odda on the back, and then pushed him away. Odda walked away quickly, whistling. He felt he had the advantage for once in his life, finally having the courage to tell McPierson off. He knew he wasn't really telling him off, but he took a great sense of self-satisfaction in finally setting the record straight. McPierson usually took the credit for everything. Maybe things would be different around town from now on. He turned toward the men, shouting, 'It was nice to meet you, Major!' He didn't wait for a response. He turned back around and kept walking.

"'You don't suppose he heard what we were saying do you?' McPierson asked.

"MacDonald grunted boisterously, 'That's absurd!'

"A Chinese man drove up in MacDonald's carriage. He stepped into the back without a word, and disappeared into the night.

"McPierson's carriage arrived within minutes. As it slowed to stop, McPierson instructed the driver to get out. He took the reins and sped off."

TWENTY-NINE

"Back inside the Swanson parlor," Eric continued, "A.P. and his son Fred sat at the table. Out-of-town guests were scattered throughout the lounge.

"'Business is down,' said A.P. in a troubled voice. 'We only have eight guests checked in, and we are approaching high season. We are going to have to let some workers go.'

"A Chinese man named John walked up to the table to retrieve the dirty dishes. A.P. fell silent.

"'Thank you, John…. Say, John—how's business at the laundry?'

"'Not so good,' John replied in broken English. 'White people afraid to come. Say want to, but still no come.'

"'How's your cousin at the store doing?'

"'Good, good. But lotta fighting upstairs, and Wong missing wife bad.'

"'That was a terrible passing,' Fred said.

"'When are you going to get your own wife?' A.P. asked, trying to lighten up the mood.

"John let out a huge laugh.

"'What's so funny?' A.P. asked. 'Am I a funny guy?'

"Fred nudged A.P. and looked around the room. It was so quiet you could hear a pin drop. Everyone in the room stared at A.P. and

Fred, who dared to converse with a Chinese servant on a social level. They glared at the two men with a vengeance. Fred looked back at all of them and stood up.

"'Good evening, everyone. My name is Fred Swanson, and this here is my father, A.P.'

"A.P. stood up and gave a half-bow and a presidential wave.

"'We want to welcome you to our establishment here. We hope you enjoy your stay in Santa Cruz. Drinks are on the house! Hit it, Tony!' Tony hopped off the barstool and removed his hat. He waltzed over to the piano and, placing the hat upside down for tips, he began to play.

"Over at Wong Kee's store, Wong kneeled, facing a lit candle, which burned continuously in front of his deceased wife's photograph. John from the Swanson's house quietly walked in. His real name was Ah Moon. He fell to his knees next to Wong. Wong looked up at the photo with tears in his eyes.

"'I miss her so much. As I look at her, I see the children we will never have. And now I am so lonely.'

"Ah Moon's eyes swelled with an ocean of sadness.

"'I am lonely, too. Feel heart broken into million pieces,' he said, holding his stomach. 'Can never put back together. Never.'

"Not many people knew the agony Ah Moon felt because he always smiled at work; he didn't want anyone to know the depth of his grief. He especially hid his feelings in front of white people—even to speak personally with a white was taboo, and he didn't want to lose his job. The Swansons were decent people—they were the most fair and polite whites he ever had worked for. In fact, they treated him like a human being and let him know they needed him."

THIRTY

As Ms. Rowanna's class continued to listen, Eric told more of his family's past.

"Major Hank MacDonald had just arrived at his Victorian manor on Beach Hill. As he unlocked the door, he thought he heard drumming in the distance—Indian drumming.

"'Now how on God's earth are those damn Indian low-lives drumming this late at night—and why are they so close?' he said aloud to himself.

"Then he dismissed the sound, thinking about his further plans for the night.

"Inside the house, he crept up the grand staircase to the second floor. Ever so carefully, he cracked open the door to his bedroom, where his wife slept soundly. He stood there and stared at her for several moments, ensuring she was in a deep sleep; he didn't want to get caught.

"Then he tiptoed down the hall to his stepdaughter's room. He cautiously turned the bedroom doorknob; he always kept it well oiled so it didn't squeak. He slowly pushed the door open and stood silently, waiting for his eyes to adjust to the dark. He wanted to see whether she was asleep, but ultimately, it didn't matter. He was only interested in relieving his wildest, most devious desires.

"He knew he had many demons, but out of all of them, including his greediness and hunger for political power, this was by far his greatest challenge. He simply could not and would not resist her.

"'Agnes,' he whispered.

"There was no answer.

"'Agnes.'

"Agnes had pulled the sheet over her head before she went to sleep. She knew he would be back for more. Just the sound of his silent force made her heart thump a thousand beats. She was sound asleep, until she heard his heavy whisper.

"'Oh, God,' she thought to herself, 'not again, not now, not tonight.'

"'Agnes,' he hastily whispered one last time as he locked the door behind him. She gasped, widely opening her eyes under the sheet, praying for Jesus to save her.

"'Please, sweet Lord, if you are really there, please don't let him touch me.'

"'Agnes, darling, don't be difficult.'

"He sat down on the edge of her bed.

"'I've been gone all night.'

"Then he spoke in an eerie, baby voice.

"'Didn't you miss your daddy?'

"His eyes turned red and glowed in the dark for a moment. The Indian drumming pounded more loudly. The demons inside the Major opened up the black void and attracted the Pogonip ghost like suction from a vacuum. It called for him, but the Major's demons silenced its scream. The Pogonip's hair flew wildly in the wind and fog outside of Agnes' bedroom window. His mouth opened wide, but the sound wouldn't come out.

"Too afraid to scream, Agnes numbed out when he ran his chunky, cold fingers across the inside of her thighs, slowly spreading them.

"Three worlds collided as the demons demanded dominance over the man, the young woman, and the Pogonip ghost. Lost between the reality of the third dimensional realm of cold earth, which the man called home and the ghost called hell, Agnes wept an ocean of hopelessness as her hands clenched the sides of her sheets so tightly she nearly ripped them to shreds."

THIRTY-ONE

Ms. Rowanna's class sat as wide-eyed as Agnes in the story as Eric continued.

"The next morning, Agnes, her mother, and the Major ate breakfast downstairs in the dinning room. Agnes stared down at the table as a Chinese man served their food.

"'Thank you, Charlie,' her mother said.

"'His name is Tam,' Agnes said. 'Why do you always call him Charlie? Or John? Or whatever? Those aren't their real names. They have their own real names. You make me sick.'

"'Are we having a problem here?' her mother asked, shocked.

"Agnes' attitude concerned her. She wondered what had gotten into her daughter. Little did she know—and wouldn't be willing to admit—her husband had gotten into Agnes.

"Thoughts raced through the mother's head. 'How can she be so horrid when she was raised with so much love and attention?'

"After her divorce, which was unheard of in those days, she knew she was lucky not only to get another chance at marriage, but also to have all of the luxuries that came along with being married to the Major.

"'Why does Agnes not see this? Was she spoiled rotten?' she wondered. 'Agnes never acted this way before the Major came into the picture. He was rich. He was powerful and very handsome. What more could she ask out of a father figure?'

"'What has gotten into you, Agnes?' her mother demanded.

"The Major interrupted.

"'She has a good point, dear.'

"Then he turned to Agnes and calmly explained that they did not have the time or the patience to learn Chinese, so that was why they called the Chinese by decent Christian names.

"'And they are grateful for that,' her mother said. 'Where is your gratitude Agnes?'

"Agnes was too tired to play games with the two of them anymore.

"'Who is *we?*' she asked the Major. 'You hate the Chinese! So why do you insist on their employment? Honestly!'

"Agnes ran out the back door to the stables to see her horse.

"'I think she's gone mad,' the Major said evenly, raising his eyebrows.

"In the stable, Agnes cried hysterically and held on tight to the neck of her horse. Of all God's creatures, she knew he could feel her pain. She couldn't help but to think, 'If the world is this hard, who needs it?' She had suffered enough loss in her life, starting with her first father. She had loved him with all of her heart. She thought about all of the hugs and laughs, and then she remembered the end.

"'How could he die on me?' she thought. 'Just losing him was enough. But now this—this horrible, hefty freak of a specimen who considers himself even close to being human, and who calls himself *my* father.'

"How could she tell her mother? It would break her heart. Her only hope was that somehow he would die, too. As much as it would hurt to see her mother in that much pain all over again, she knew it would be for the best.

"Later on that afternoon, Agnes sat under a cypress tree at Lighthouse Field. The trees grew from roots centuries old. The sky was a deep, dark blue, and it was monarch butterfly season. Bright orange and black wings fluttered around her, swooping and dancing for their mates.

"Agnes rode her horse there habitually. And she never went anywhere without her adored setter. She bathed her dog in the finest perfume on a regular basis. With her horse grazing in the sweet grass nearby and the dog by her side, she lay in the deep, soft grass, soaking her face in the warming winter sunlight.

"Looking up to the tops of the trees with a smile on her face, dozens of butterflies circled around in the soft morning fog. This was her refuge. She felt like nothing could ever go wrong in the world when she was there. It was like a dream.

"What Agnes failed to notice were the Indian ghosts enjoying the same blessed, sacred space, from a time history had let slip away. But then, in that very special moment, there was no such thing as time, only the space they shared, the beauty and the love. Young Ohlone Indian children chased the butterflies, giggling as the elders, who sat wisely on their horses, watched over their sanctuary. Lighthouse Field provided a safe haven for them all. It was a sphere that shielded all negativity and wielded off the dark souls of the land of the lost. Only the purest of reason and disposition came there for healing. And so it was."

THIRTY-TWO

Just then the bell rang at Santa Cruz High. The students jumped out of their seats. Everyone knew what to expect from the class by then: the unexpected. The whole situation was so surreal, but for some reason, everyone went with the flow. Besides, what alternative did they have? And anyway, they didn't know anything about Santa Cruz history—no one else talked about it. And how could they complain about their class? No one would believe the experiences they shared in classroom number nine.

"Thank you, Eric; that will be enough for today. My goodness, you really paint a vivid picture of Santa Cruz history," said Rowanna. "You could write a book."

"Thank you!" Eric said as Leslie walked by and smiled at him. "I've gotta go. Have a nice day, Ms. Rowanna!"

Eric dropped the photos he had brought to class and chased after Leslie. When he finally caught up to her, he didn't have anything in particular to say to her. All he knew was he just wanted to be with her.

"Hi, ahhh, I was wondering if you would like to, ahhh…" then it popped in his head: "go for a hike up in Felton with me?"

"Really? I would love to!" Leslie had wondered whether he was ever going to ask her out. She didn't care what it was—the thought of being with him made her happy. She dug around in her huge purse, searching for a pen and something to write on. She pushed away various photos of people and places she loved, a phone book, old concert and movie ticket stubs, tampons, make-up, a bottle of lightly-scented body oil called "Rain," some breath mints, a brush, and a couple of mismatched earrings.

"Look, I'll just come and pick you up at 10:00 tomorrow. Will that work for you?" Eric asked, saving her the trouble of finding something to write on.

"Perfect! See you then!"

She started to waltz off, then stopped.

"Hey! You don't have my address!"

"Oh, yeah; what is it?"

"The corner of Columbia and Bay—yellow house on the right. You can't miss it. I'll be outside."

"I'll be there."

Eric was sure this was the best thing ever to happen to him. He wondered whether he'd put his arm around her, whether he'd kiss her. He could hardly think straight, when all of a sudden he bumped into Viper.

"Wow, dude, slow down there," Viper said.

Eric felt like an idiot.

"Sorry."

"Wanna go to a party at a haunted house up on Front Street tonight?"

"Hell, yeah! I'll be there!" Eric said.

Viper stuck out his two index fingers and pointed them straight at Eric.

"You're the man." And he swooped off like a bat out of sight.

Eric started talking to himself.

"Okay, I'm the man…. Damn right, I'm the man. The man who is going to get laid by the woman of his dreams. I am the man, I am the man, I AM THE MAN!"

He let out a "Yeah, baby," as Randy walked up.

"What in the hell are you doing, and what did that asshole want?"

"Party. At the haunted house up on Front Street. Tonight."

"Oh, hell, yes, I am all over it!"

Randy slapped Eric's hand bro-style.

"Brother from another mother, you're the man; you are the man and don't forget it!" said Randy.

"I am the man, aren't I?"

Eric started to believe his own publicity. Randy started to sing.

"We gonna part-ay. We gonna part-ay, uh huh, uh huh, uh huh, uh huh...." Then he pointed to his pants and grabbed his package and thrust his pelvis. "Put it here, put it here, put it here, put it here..."

Just then, Howard and Giliano timidly walked past.

"Hey, I have to talk to you," Randy shouted to Howard. Howard hurried past Randy without looking up.

"Hey, I am talking to you!" Randy sounded aggressive, but he didn't mean to. Howard sped up—he thought for sure he was doomed, again. Randy ran after him and grabbed him by the sleeve. "Hey, I need to talk to you."

Howard stopped and looked down at the ground, shaking. Giliano stepped between them.

"What do you want." It wasn't a question; it was a threat. Well, the best threat Giliano could give Randy. His right eye started to twitch, and he couldn't stop blinking his eyes. It was a nervous habit. Just the same, he rolled up his sleeves and stuck up his dukes.

"One of us is going down, and it's probably going to be me," Giliano said. "But you see now, I don't care anymore because you have left me with no other choice."

"Step aside, 'Ragu,'" said Randy. "This is between me and Howard."

Randy dug around in his pocket and pulled out a shiny coin with a hole in the middle of it. He held it out as an offering to Howard.

"Please take it. After my mother died, I was given a small bag with some of her personal belongings in it. I kept it in my top drawer, way in the back, under my socks. I didn't look inside of it until the other day. I was scared. I didn't want to feel close to her because she was already gone. This coin is special and extremely rare. I don't know if it's worth much, but it means everything to me. It's from a Chinese dynasty. It was made during the reign of the Kangxi Emperor sometime between 1654 and 1722 in the Qing dynasty. Most coins were made from copper, brass, or iron. This one here is gold. Please take it."

Howard couldn't believe it. He was a coin collector. The corners of his lips began to quiver and he fought them to stop himself from crying. His nose started to drip, and as he sniffled, he wondered whether there was some kind of catch. He couldn't say anything, but he felt forgiveness in his heart toward Randy.

No one knew the hardships his own family had been through, being one of the first Chinese to land in San Francisco so long ago. They were the first to build forts and take shelter and refuge in Santa Cruz once they found out there was no place for the Chinese to prosper in digging gold. His parents were the first to attend a university.

So he just stood there. Randy picked up his hand and placed the coin in Howard's palm and firmly squeezed his hand shut.

"I am Chinese as well, my brother. I hated you because I hated myself. But I'll have your back from here on out."

And with that, Randy ran after Eric.

"Whoa, there; are you serious? What the hell, dude? This is good. This is really good," Eric said.

"The only one you need Randy to have your back for is from him!" said Giliano.

Then he saw the look on Howard's face. So humble. So relieved.

"I'm sorry," said Giliano. He didn't want to rob him of the moment, so he lied. "I am happy for you. Let's get out of here."

Back in the classroom, Rowanna found the stack of photos Eric had dropped as he rushed out of class. He was long gone now, so she picked them up and put them in her purse. She figured they would be safer at her house than with the janitors. Plus, she could look through them when she got home; she didn't think Eric would mind.

Randy and Eric parked at the Steamer's Lane to surf. They had already squeezed into their tight, thick, wetsuits to endure the chilly water. They were gazing at the water to see how the waves looked when Randy saw something going on over at the lighthouse. It was a group of at least twenty-five to thirty people who appeared to be gathered for a funeral. Everyone was wearing black and everyone was black.

"Isn't that Thomas over there?"

"Huh?" Eric replied.

"Thomas. He's over there. Look."

Thomas' mother started to wail and flung herself, full-body on the grass. She held a small wooden shoebox. Thomas was trying to pry it away from her. "Holy crap! We have to find out what happened!" Eric said.

Everyone wore white carnations or orchid corsages. Off to the side, a group of six guys dressed in tuxedos stood in a row, holding a bouquet of black balloons to launch. Each one had a can of Budweiser beer in his hand, but no one was smiling. A little girl with pigtails tied tightly to her head held a basket of daisies, which she dropped at people's feet. As Thomas' mother pulled herself together, a couple of ladies brushed off pieces of grass stuck to her dress. They joined in a circle and held hands as a thin, bald-headed man, dressed in a stiff, white suit, carried a cage of white doves to the center of the circle.

Eric and Randy drew in closer to the scene.

It was shocking because they had no idea what had happened.

Thomas was "one of them." One of their best buddies of all time. Why hadn't he told them something serious had happened? They approached Thomas.

"Hey, buddy, what's going on here?" Eric asked.

Thomas was distant and distraught.

"My father. He's in the box. What's left of him."

"What?" Randy asked. "How can this be?"

"Everything I ever was and ever will be is in this box," Thomas said. "He was my hero."

After a moment, he continued, "Remember the foot? Remember your funny foot story, Randy?"

An acidic feeling poured through Randy's stomach lining; he felt compelled to deny everything.

"What are you talking about? I just saw him the other day at Garfield Park."

Randy buckled over and almost puked.

"Oh, God. How did this happen?" Eric asked.

The man opened up the cage and dozens of white doves flew to their freedom as the pastor delivered his final eulogy. Then the guys in tuxedos released the seventy-two black balloons and guzzled their beers. "Amazing Grace" began to play on a loud speaker from someone's truck as Thomas' mother cried out to the Lord one last time for mercy.

THIRTY-THREE

Tim came home after a long day at the school. He was physically exhausted from just standing around all day—standing in the hallway, at the courtyard, in the parking lot, behind the bush, in the bathrooms. All day he took notes and tried to look important, radioing to no one in particular on his walkie-talkie and watching, waiting. Not much ever happened at the school, so he wondered, "Why did they even bother hiring a security guard?" Most of the students behaved well, except for that vile kid, Randy. Tim began to feel worthless, but he wondered where to go from here. What would he do next?

He threw his dark blue security jacket over a chair in the kitchen, grabbed a root beer, and turned on the TV. A commercial aired with a song he liked so much that he turned it up and sat down just to listen to it. It was Sarah McLachlan singing "In the Arms of an Angel."

The commercial was for the Humane Society. Faces of baby cats and dogs, one after another, showed up on the screen, abused and battered. The camera zoomed in to a baby kitten's sick, drooping eyes. The sight tore Tim's heart out. The commercial lingered on. It was like an infomercial from hell or something. The longer he watched, the more torn up he got. He hadn't felt sadness like this as an adult.

He remembered a time way back when he found a small, wet kitten after a street fight he'd had back east. He took it home and fed it a can of tuna. The cat was so hungry it ate the top of the plastic fork he fed it with. After he picked a dozen or so fleas off of it, he wrapped its tiny little body in a dry wash rag, and they both fell fast asleep. The next morning, he found the kitten dead from severe dehydration. The fact that he couldn't save it broke his heart. He never forgot about it.

The song played quietly in the background while Sarah spoke softly. "You can help these animals in need. With your love and kindness, we can turn things around and make a difference for these precious angels of ours. You can make a difference in the world. All they want to do is love us, protect us, and be loved. Pick up the phone and call now."

The song grew louder again.

Tim dug into his pocket and grabbed his notepad and pen. He watched until the phone number came up on the screen. He began to get choked up when finally the number appeared. He wrote it down, walked into the bathroom, and took a long, hard look at himself.

"What if what Holly said is true?"

He felt his face soften around the edges.

"Maybe the world isn't as hard and cruel as I thought," he said to himself. His eyes brightened. Maybe his life really was getting better. He took a deep breath, slowly in through the nose and out through the mouth, and felt a sudden release. He began to laugh and ripped the toupee off of his head.

He scurried to the front door, flung it wide open, and ran out without his jacket. He flew down the rickety old stairs leading to the dark alley and shouted:

"I'm free! I'm free!"

Then he jumped in his car and went to the Capitola Mall for some new clothes and a haircut.

THIRTY-FOUR

Rowanna opened the envelope that Eric had forgotten in the classroom. She looked at a photo of a smoldering building engulfed in flames dated May 31st, 1887.

Rowanna could feel herself slipping into the photo. It was one of her deepest, darkest secrets: She possessed the gift of premonition and clarity so strongly that other dimensions of time literally sucked her in. It could be the future, but in this case, it was the past. It happened to her in class, but she didn't yet realize the same thing was happening to her students.

Regardless, she didn't consider it a gift. She wanted more than anything just to be normal. She found it painful and frightening to journey to the places she went. And most of the time, she couldn't stop it.

As she slipped deeper and further away from the present, she found herself in the presence of William Swanson, A.P.'s brother and Fred's uncle. She watched him ransack the Swanson parlor. The family had questioned his sanity for some time, and they were considering putting him into a sanitarium.

Just weeks before, they had found him curled up in a fetal position, sucking his thumb and twirling his fingers around in his hair on a corner in the middle of Front Street.

Before that, he had got drunk and started flinging food at the Swanson's parlor in front of some wealthy and highly influential bankers from San Francisco. He laughed while the guests moved out to another boarding house and swore never to come back.

When they returned to San Francisco, they spread the word about their horrid experience at The Swanson Boarding House.

Emma watched him curiously from a doorway. She spoke to him slowly and clearly.

"What are you doing, Uncle Bill?"

"I'm looking for something."

"Maybe I know where it is," Emma said. "Would you like to tell me what it is you are looking for?"

"Matches," he said in a high-pitched voice. "I am looking for matches!"

She pointed them out, on the fireplace mantel.

"What was I thinking, thinking, thinking? Ah, oh, I just lost it!"

He lunged for the fireplace and grabbed a handful of matches, and then ran out the front door. Emma chased after him.

"Uncle Bill! Where are you going?"

She couldn't see him in the dark, so she fetched Fred.

"Did you see which way he headed?" Fred asked. "Did he say anything else?"

"Yes," Emma said. "He said he never should have sold out."

A.P. and Fred eventually found William at the old Pescadero Swanson ranch house. The new owners peered through the kitchen window. Fred gave them the heads up, and they waved him over to the back of the barn. It wasn't the first time this had happened. The drunken William Swanson had shown up many times, most of the time just to sit somewhere on the property to drink and reminiscence about the good old days.

William had bought the land and built the ranch before anyone made it out West. He was the first Swanson to arrive in Santa Cruz. He had grown old, and the family had talked him into selling the property, against his wishes. He had regretted it ever since. Holding a bottle of whiskey in one hand and a handful of matches in the other, he held the old Swanson Pescadero ranch sign under his arm and cried.

"Why did we sell it? The ranch was all I ever did right—it was all I ever did, period."

Fred said, "Oh, Uncle Billy, don't ya see? You were the greatest! But like all good things, everything must come to an end. We didn't have the skills you had to run the ranch. We moved onto business and enterprise. We were losing too much money and almost lost everything just keeping it going."

"But it's not the end, end," A.P. said. He eyeballed Fred and wondered why he said that. It only made it worse, and it seemed like a lie. But he wanted to encourage his big brother, even if it was a lie.

"Of course it's not the end." Fred stumbled on his words.

"Why, it's just the beginning, the beginning of something else is all."

Fred wiped the sweat off his brow while William took a hard swig on his bottle and settled back on the barn's edge.

"Do what you want with me. A man works his whole life thinkin' somethin' big is gonna happen. Then nothin' happens. I don't know what's spoze to, just somethin'—anything. And then you just get old, and it's just like that. Boom. Thank you very much ladies and gentleman. You don't mind if I die now, do you? Please, someone put me out of my misery. I never did much that amounted to anything anyway."

Bill was exhausted from a long hard life. And he was depressed and not thinking straight. He failed to see all of the helpful things he did for his family. He took another swig off his bottle.

"I'm a done deal."

Fred edged in another word. "Don't you see, Uncle Billy? If it weren't for you, none of us would even be here. You were the first one here—the first Swanson in Santa Cruz. Do you realize what you started? I'll never let you down, Uncle Billy; you'll see."

Fred wiped his wet eyes with his white cotton sleeve. The words nearly brought him to his knees; he knew everything they owned had resulted from his uncle's tireless efforts. All three of them sat slumped behind the old barn. Fred grabbed the bottle and took a drink and then passed the bottle to his father. A.P. took a sip, gagged, and passed it back to William.

They remained, talking to William for some time, hoping to knock some sense into him. Meanwhile, the new owners wandered curiously around the property, hoping to hear a glimpse of the three men's conversation.

Not long after, down at Hong Lee's Laundry, someone lit a match, which started a fire. Within minutes, the fire spread throughout town, and people scrambled for safety.

On May 31st, 1887, *The Sentinel* revealed the story on the front page.

"The Swanson House, along with six other structures—The Swiss Hotel, the Wash House of Hong Lee, Goodwins Stables, The Santa Cruz House, the Franklin House, and The Eagle Stables—were consumed."

The next day, A.P. Swanson was on his knees, bent over in the dirt where The Swanson Boarding House stood just one day before.

"How could this be?" thought Fred. He stood close, with his hand on his father's shoulder. The entire family huddled together.

Throughout town, groups of families stood in disbelief, looking at the charred rubble of their family livelihood. Rumor had it that the old Swanson man, who was close to suicide anyway, started the fire. The old man sat on the side of the curb with his head tucked in his knees, rocking. Officers finally took him away, but no one could ever prove he was the one who lit the fire, and little was ever said about it again.

Strangely enough, another fire ripped through the city of Santa Cruz seven years later, in April 1894, taking the Courthouse, The Eagle Stable, The Hoataling, The Staller, The Vahlberg, The Leonard, The Werner, The Simpson, The Rice, The Girabaldi, and The Went building. Others sustained damage. That afternoon, a main water gate at the reservoir burst, cutting off the water supply to downtown. The people of Santa Cruz wondered whether it was mere coincidence.

THIRTY-FIVE

Rowanna picked up another photo of Swanson waving to hundreds of people. He had become a public figure in Santa Cruz.

Rowanna fell into the photo, as if she were there. She could see it was nine years later. Hundreds of people lined the streets. Outside The Old Fellows Building, six hundred lights spelled out the words "Big Creek Power." People carried Fred Swanson up to the balcony to give a speech commemorating the event. As everyone yelled, "Speech! Speech!" Fred only had one thing to say: "The lights speak for themselves!" As if on cue, the town band began to play.

The next day, the second annual Venetian Water Carnival drew thousands of people from all over. There were boats covered with flowers and people waving as they floated past.

After the Southern Pacific Railroad train pulled in, mobs of people poured out. Girls wore cool, white skirts and straw sailor hats. The young men donned ducks and flannels. People wove in and out of the crowds, which moved in all directions. Rowanna could hear the clanking of brass bands and the hissing of rockets.

Residents dressed the entire town in yellow and white. From balcony to balcony and house to house top, yellow and white garlands adorned the streets. Long strips of cambric wound around the wheels of express wagons.

"Fifteen thousand showed up last year!" Fred said to his father.

"Yes, but we were in debt for months after that," his father replied.

"But the local merchants made tons of money!"

"I'm talking about the city, Fred," his father said.

Fred smiled. "This city hasn't seen anything yet!"

Fred was friendly with the visitors—just like a politician—and they responded accordingly.

"Welcome to Santa Cruz!" Fred said to everyone he could, shaking hands.

Rowanna snapped out of the scene and looked at the next photo. It depicted Fred and his wife, Emma, in front of a colorful riverfront, with lights hanging everywhere. The couple attended a house party in Capitola that evening. As they enjoyed the aquatic parade in its glowing, nighttime glory in the black river water, a live orchestra played. Lantern lights, Roman candles, and flowers added to the ambiance. Champagne flowed as Fred and Emma gazed at the water silently. They both knew they had the world at their feet, as well as one another. Emma spoke tenderly to her husband.

"Our life is like a dream."

"There are so many things to do and so little time," Fred responded hastily.

"Oh, Fred, can't you just stop for one minute and enjoy some of it?"

"What's not to enjoy?" he said, as he held her closely in his arms.

A couple walked past them and stopped for a moment.

"Good job at Big Creek!" the gentleman said.

"Thank you," Fred said. "Why thank you very much! There's more where that came from!"

"Fred," Emma said, tugging gently on his arm.

"What?"

She looked away.

"What did I do?" Fred asked.

She moved away from him.

"What don't you do? The opera house, the baseball field, all of the games, the railroad, the telephones—you do too much. I need more time with you. People want to know when you sleep. I tell them you hang upside down in the closet for an hour, and that's about it."

He chuckled heartily and remembered why he married Emma in the first place. She was beautiful, talented, and the funniest woman he had ever met.

As passionately as he could say it, he whispered, "It is difficult getting any shuteye sleeping next to you."

"Oh, Fred."

She gushed with affection and moved closer to him. They engaged in a long kiss.

Two teenage girls walked by, staring.

"Oh, Fred, I love you."

"I love you too, my queen."

"I thought Santa Cruz was your queen," Emma said, teasingly.

"You're my real queen, darling. I will always love you first and foremost."

They both gazed at the trail of boats lit up with candles and lights. Fireworks exploded with color in the sky.

THIRTY-SIX

Rowanna picked up a photo of Fred Swanson and a group of businessmen standing in a circle, shaking hands over a table. She rubbed the photo and held it to her heart as she slipped off into the past.

It featured an ambitious man, who was moving up in the world at the Superior Court Room of the City Hall. It was early evening. He was proposing the realization of his dream—to establish a West Coast Coney Island, right there at the waterfront of Santa Cruz.

In addition to the county board of directors, H.R. Judah, "Passenger Agent" for the Southern Pacific Railroad, attended the meeting. He had supported tourism in Santa Cruz all along.

"As everyone here knows, last summer was a huge success," Fred said.

"For eighty days straight, we booked the best bands available, every night. We have had nightly fireworks, a huge Fourth of July celebration, nightly illumination on the streets throughout downtown, and, to top it off, our beloved president of the United States, Mr. Theodore Roosevelt, is on his way to visit our fine city.

"Let me remind everyone in this room that I did not get one red cent for my work over the summer as Director General of the New Santa Cruz Committee.

"However, I did receive $153 in expenses for traveling around the state to engage bands. Now with this out of the way, let's get to the main part of the meeting."

Judah stood up for the committee and spoke.

"The Southern Pacific Company will do everything in its power to promote the project and take extraordinary means to advertise it."

He sat back down.

Fred introduced Mr. C. Ackerman.

"Mr. Ackerman?"

Ackerman stood up and unrolled a display for everyone to see. Fred went on with his typical showman style.

"Lady," he said, looking at the secretary, who was the only female in attendance, "and gentlemen: As most of you know, this is Mr. Ackerman, the artist for the *Sunset Magazine*."

Ackerman pulled a huge cloth off of an easel, and the members gasped.

"There will be an Oriental style bathhouse, a pagoda shaped pavilion, and a grand tent city," Fred explained.

Ackerman took over from there.

"We will build a casino with a roof garden surrounded by bathhouses on each side. The tent city will be constructed where the Dolphin Park is. We will also dam the San Lorenzo River to create a lake. In the center of the lake, we will erect a bandstand and dance pavilion. This structure will connect to the mainland by a large bridge."

It was Fred's turn to speak.

"I've already placed the Miller and the Leibrandt Neptune Baths in escrow. First, we will raise $40,000 to $50,000 from local subscription."

The financing annoyed members of the committee.

"The remainder of the estimated cost of $200,000 will be raised by holding a land sale to sell off the lots in the tent city," Fred said, ignoring the grumbling.

"There will be excursions from all parts of the state during the sale of the lots. After all of this, we will build a large hotel. Construction will be in this order because we must cater to the masses!"

The last statement pleased committee members, and Fred seized the opportunity to introduce his new partners on the endeavor. Some of them already sat on the Common Council committee.

"My colleagues, my friends," Fred said with great emphasis, "I would like to introduce to you Mr. H. Whiley, Mr. T.W. Kelley, Mr. F.R. Walti, and Mr. H.E. Irish."

Each man stood up as Fred introduced him.

"Everyone: We are the Santa Cruz Beach Cottage and Tent City Corporation!"

THIRTY-SEVEN

Rowanna picked up yet another photo. It was dated Saturday, June 12, 1904. It depicted the opening of the casino. The *U.S.S. Albatross* sat in front of the casino in the bay. Fred couldn't help but think it was one of the most impressive sights he had ever encountered. Exactly at noon, the powerhouse whistle blew. Every flag on the thirty-six poles of the casino fluttered up the halyard and flew in the breeze. Fred held his daughter Pearl in his arms while his wife stood close by. He realized Santa Cruz was, and would always be, the Queen of the Summer Resorts.

That night the champagne flowed, and everyone who was an "anyone" attended the gala, greeting Fred and his wife.

"I can't believe this is happening," Emma said quietly.

"What? You're not happy?" Fred murmured as he waved to guests.

"Very funny," she said.

Cottardo Peter Rapallino entered with his wife, Maria, and their three sons, Cottardo II, Malio, and Malio II.

"Rapallino, and your lovely wife, Maria," Fred greeted them.

Rapallino had a thick Italian accent.

"You gotta everything here," Rapallino said. "You need-a more fish, you let me know." Rapallino was a fisherman. "We got tons of salmon, sea bass, rock cod, sole, and sable. So fresh, melt in your mouth like a succulent lemon chocolate."

Malio II pulled on his father's arms.

"Daddy! Daddy! I want to go to the pool! Please, Daddy!"

Maria reprimanded Rapallino in Italian as she pulled him away from Fred. As they walked away, Fred could hear her say "Grazie" harshly.

Major Hank MacDonald arrived with his wife. He held Margaret in one arm and now full-grown Agnes in the other.

"I'm impressed, Swanson. You did good this time."

He looked around.

"Very good."

Agnes looked around in amazement. Some of her friends walked in behind them. They all hugged each other, jumping up and down. Agnes tried to control herself.

"We must contain ourselves, girls; we are grown up women now!" Agnes giggled so hard she had to cover her mouth. Her friends pressed down their skirts.

"Of course," one of her friends said.

"I don't know what's gotten into us!" They laughed. "Where's the champagne?" another friend asked.

"Let's go find it, girls," Emma said, grabbing Agnes' arm. "This way."

Agnes turned to her mother. "You'll be okay, won't you?"

Her mother nodded. MacDonald gave her a disapproving look. Agnes turned and walked away. She then turned back around to him again, as if in slow motion, and gave him the "evil eye."

The casino brimmed with life with gambling tables, live music, a bar, and a huge buffet, including a champagne table outside in one of the gardens. The ladies took their drinks and mingled. Emma saw Dudley McPierson.

"Mr. McPierson!"

"Why, hello, Emma. I have to admit it: This must be the party of the century."

Ernest Odda was standing there.

"You can say that again!"

A photographer snapped some shots. Fred walked up. "Yes! The party of the century! But don't forget; it's only 1904!"

They all laughed. Then suddenly, a fireworks display captivated their attention. It sprawled over the *U.S.S. Albatross* and what looked like the entire Monterey Bay.

Farther away from the scene, at the mouth of the San Lorenzo River, there was something else going on. Sea lions barked. The moon was full, and the lights illuminated the rocky cliffs. A group of what was left of the Ohlone Indians gathered, dressed in full apparel. With only the sound of the sea lions barking and light drumming, tears streamed down their cheeks as they silently gazed at the casino.

Suddenly, Rowanna was sucked back into her body. She was exhausted. It had been a long night; she had practically re-lived more than a decade of Fred Swanson's life. She slipped on her old raggedy light-blue nightgown and went to bed with her cats.

THIRTY-EIGHT

Tim was sitting in a hair salon chair for the first time in his life. He had three large department store bags filled with new clothing—all black—of course. Hip-hop music played loudly, and all he could smell was something fruity—or cucumber; he couldn't tell for sure. He only knew it emanated from the goop the redheaded lady wearing a ton of make-up had applied to his hair. She would have been attractive if it weren't for her two chins and skinny chicken legs.

She handed him a mirror and spun him around on the chair to see what he thought of the back.

"Wow," she said. "You look great in black. Has anyone ever told you that?"

Tim took a look at his new style.

"I just can't believe it. I had no idea how different it would look."

"Yeah," she said. "Everyone's shaving their heads these days. You look fantastic."

She started rubbing his head, first in what seemed to be a professional manner, but as she kept rubbing and rubbing around his crown, it seemed like she was holding his head in a controlling, dominant manner. She pressed into him and pulled something from out of her gigantic breasts.

"Here's my card; if you ever want to go out for a drink or something, sometime."

It was the first time in years anyone had even given him the time of day. Tim looked shocked, which gave her the impression he might already have someone.

"Oh, I mean, that is if you're not already attached," she said.

"Attached?" he said. "To what?"

He didn't know what that meant. He knew that her breasts were attached to him, literally. He felt cornered like animal prey, so he asked her whether she liked animals, just to change the subject. Anyway, he did want to know whether she liked animals, because after watching the sad commercial, he had decided to commit his life to working with animals.

"Not really, sweetie. I got four kids at home and an estranged husband."

"Oh," said Tim. "That's nice. Well, I better get going."

That was the last thing he wanted to get involved with. He'd done time with guys like her husband. And he didn't want any trouble from husbands. He left her card on the table with a five-dollar tip.

"You forgot my card," she shouted as he walked out, but he just kept walking.

Anyone can shave an almost-bald head, he thought. He would find someone else to do it next time.

He wandered into a coffee shop with a bookstore. Or was it a bookstore that had a coffee shop? "Good God, things are complicated in California," he thought to himself.

He ordered a hot chocolate with extra whipped cream and wandered through the aisles, blowing lightly on the sides of the blistering hot top of the cup. Every once in awhile, he was able to suck up a little of the whipped cream, being careful not to burn his lip.

A book cover with two guys hanging by their necks over a bridge caught his eye. He read the title of the thin book: *The Water Street Bridge*.

"I wonder if it's based on a true story," Tim thought. "It is in the history section, after all."

He sauntered over to a dark purple squishy chair, sunk into it, and placed the hot cup on the table. He read the first few lines of the book:

"On May 3, 1877, it was a thick and foggy morning in Santa Cruz. Two bodies were hanging off of the Water Street Bridge. Rigor mortis had already set in by the time people found them. Soon, a crowd formed and started to ask questions."

"Oh, yeah," Tim said aloud. "This is going to be gu-u-oood." He kept reading:

"Five days earlier, a sixty-two-year old, Henry De Forrest, was walking along River Street from a long hard day's work at the California Powder Works construction site. Two guys with hoods approached him. They shot him with a large caliber revolver, but he wasn't dead yet. They proceeded to drag him quite a ways while he begged for his life. His wife and children were on their way from Maine to live there. One of the black-hooded men pulled out his pockets and took all of Henry's belongings. They left him there in a pool of blood, dead.

"Jose 'Chumales' Gonzales was twenty-one years old. He lived at his Indian-Mexican mother's home in Watsonville. Living the life of a half-breed took a toll on him, as well as others like him.

"People labeled him a social outcast and a deviant. He became the scapegoat for many crimes. After Henry's death, county sheriff deputies snooped around Jose's yard. They kicked around a few chickens and then burst through the front door and thrashed the entire house with no just cause. Jose held his mother close and tried to calm her down. They arrested him as his mother begged for his release. When Jose asked what they wanted from him, they never said a word; they just took him away. His mother fell to the ground in hysterics.

"Nearby, at a grassy area under a tree, Francisco Arias was camped out with two women having a ménage à trois. The deputies hid under a tree as they watched. The first deputy pulled out a blade of grass and sucked on it.

"'Well, now, isn't that a sight to see?'

"The second deputy reached into his pants and stroked his genitalia.

"'My, my, my, this fellow knows how to live.'

"The first deputy spit out the soggy lump of grass.

"'Now we are going to see if he knows how to die.'

"They moved in on the action and tied Arias up. Then they raped the women and arrested Arias.

"Later that evening in jail, both Jose and Arias sat with an Anglo and a Spanish-speaking person. They informed the two young men of exactly what they did wrong. The Anglo told Arias to say he pulled the trigger on Henry De Forrest. They convinced Jose and Arias to take the blame for the death, and since their records were worse, they didn't have much of a choice. Arias pounded his fist into his hardened hand, shaking his head and wiping the tears from his eyes. The Spanish translator told Jose to say that he 'didn't stop him.' In fact, the Spanish man said, 'You stayed on the lookout and you received approximately two dollars and fifty cents.'

"Jose threw up his arms in despair. Once again, they were nailed for something they had nothing to do with. But someone had to take the blame.

"As the townspeople slept that night, several hooded men entered the jail. They gagged the men's mouths and carried Jose and Arias out to the bridge. A group, also wearing hoods and holding candles, waited to witness the lynching. The sound of drumming rose in the distance. Jose and Arias struggled to get free, but the men tied them up by their hands and feet. Arias accepted his fate more easily than Jose, who had dreams of working hard and taking care of his mother. He thought of his mother, all alone. Jose's eyes welled up, and he began to weep.

"A Pogonip scream howled from the nearby river in the wet, dark air as the men dropped to their deaths. The hooded men listened to the squeaking of ropes twisting and stretching as the bodies spasmodically jerked from side to side, finally swaying and settling. A couple of white hands reached out to untie the cloth stuffed in the men's mouths, and one by one, the crowd dissipated.

"The next day around mid-morning, people—a lot of people—gathered around the bodies. They were bidding on the ropes, cut in one-foot lengths, for souvenirs.

"'Do I hear two pennies?' the bidder yelled out.

"'Two pennies!' a bidder shouted.

"'Do I hear five pennies? Five pennies! Sold, to the lucky winner!'

"A small child ran up to fetch his prize and said, 'Gee, thanks!' No one ever questioned what happened that night—no one asked, and no one told. Truth is, no one cared because they were half-breed Mexican Indians."

"Excuse me sir, we are closing now," a female store clerk said to Tim. "Are you going to buy that book?"

"What?" Tim asked.

The irritated clerk with a hot-pink Mohawk and a green smock stared at him, waiting for a response. "We are closed now. Everyone is gone but you. Do you want the book or not? I want to go home. I pulled a double shift here today—I've been here since eight this morning."

"Oh, I ahhh...I just read the whole thing. Do I have to buy it?"

"No. No you do not have to buy the book. Goodnight."

Tim had lost track of time. He couldn't believe the story was true.

"Listen: Yes, I would like to take the book home," he said.

She rolled her eyes as he followed her to the register.

"What time does the mall close?"

"Now. Nine o'clock. Every night except Sundays, when we close at five—sharp."

"Okey-dokey, then. Thank you," Tim said after he paid and he walked out the door, whistling to the tune of Carlos Santana's hit, "Black Magic Woman."

THIRTY-NINE

Rowanna could only sleep a couple of hours. She awoke to make tea and look at another of Eric's photos.

It was a shot of Agnes and her mother in front of their villa on Beach Hill. They smiled for the camera, but as soon as the shutter closed, they dropped the pretense. As Rowanna held the picture in her hand, she felt an agonizing pain in her head and heart.

She watched Agnes, bundled up in a robe and slippers, knock on her mother's bedroom door. But there was no answer.

"That's strange," Agnes thought to herself. Her mother always woke up before everyone else. Agnes knocked even harder, and finally opened the door.

"Mother!"

Her mother looked pale, and gray surrounded her eyes, as if she were half dead. Agnes rushed to her side. Her mother's long, thin arm dangled over the side of the bed. Her mother mumbled something.

"What, Mom?"

"I always knew," her mother replied weakly.

Agnes held her mother close to her.

"Knew what?" Agnes paused for a minute. "Why didn't you stop him?"

Tears fell from her mother's eyes, down her frozen face.

"I didn't know how. After your father died, everything was in a shambles. I was lost, and then he came along and seemed to make everything better. I was afraid to lose it all again. I figured it was better than nothing at all, which is what we would have had if it were not for him."

Agnes began to weep in her mother's arms.

"I never meant for you to have to pay so tremendously," her mother said, holding her. "I didn't know what to do. Please forgive me, Agnes, my love, my sweet little darling. Oh, Baby, please forgive me."

Not long after, Agnes' mother passed away. She died on November 16, 1905. The funeral horrified Agnes—not only was her mother gone, but now she was stuck with her stepfather, all alone. The chapel bells rang, as the Major stood outside, expressionless. After the service, he stole his wife's body and hid it in a vault, intending to investigate her true cause of death. Her death certificate blamed it on locomotor ataxia, a progressive deterioration of the spinal cord, from which she had suffered for years. But the Major never quite believed it. He didn't even have her body embalmed, and he never found an answer he could accept.

FORTY

Rowanna picked up another photo. It smelled like charcoal. "How peculiar," she thought. One of her cats meowed and moved away from it.

Fred sat at home, opening his mail. One letter read: "We are tired of you. If you don't stop promoting streetcar railways, electric light plants, and casinos, you will be called upon by a committee and tarred and feathered. — A Citizen."

Emma walked in and saw Fred's face. She grabbed the letter out of his hand.

"Not again! I want you to turn this over to the authorities, Fred; please. I'm really scared."

Fred made Santa Cruz famous. On the casino's opening day, three hundred tents stood, painted in multicolored candy stripes. Hundreds of people crowded the streets. Within the Neptune Casino stood the Neptune Grill and The Plunge—two saltwater pools, complete with skydives and slides, kept at eighty degrees. Fred had built the flushing station, which exchanged four hundred gallons per minute. Fred was getting ready to jump off of a high dive at The Plunge. His daughter, Pearl, swam around the shallow end, encouraging him to jump.

"Come on, Daddy! We are all waiting!"

Everyone in the pool started to chant.

"Jump! Jump! Jump!"

"But I'm frightened!" Fred yelled down to the bathers.

No one could tell whether he was teasing or not, but they continued to coax him.

"Okay, if you say so!"

Swanson did a double flip before he hit the water. Everyone cheered. He popped his head out of the water for a breath.

·"We are going to have a race. Whoever wins gets one free week of unlimited swimming here at The Plunge!"

As people cheered, an eerie voice emerged from the crowd. "What do you get out of it, Fred?"

Fred looked around to see who had said that, but no one was near him, until a lone swimmer came over to him.

"Are you okay?"

"Yeah, sure, I'm fine," he said in classic style, looking around one last time before he got out of the water.

Outside of The Neptune, the entire beach was filled with bands, balloons, flags, a miniature train ride, a merry-go-round, fishponds, ice cream parlors, a glass-bottom boat, a roller rink— and thousands of people.

A mother dropped her five-year-old son off at the beach. "You be good, James. Don't talk to any strangers, okay?"

"Please don't leave me, Mommy!" He began to cry. "I'm scared."

She said, "I have to go to work, son. I will be back in a few hours to get you."

She walked away from him backwards, watching him as long as she could until she reached her workplace at The Plunge. She yelled from a distance.

"I'll bring you a big treat," she yelled from a distance. "Don't talk to anyone!"

"Okay, Mommy." He turned to the ocean, the only thing he had to watch over him every day. The sweet smell of the clear, dark-green water wafted in and out upon the shore. As waves rolled away and disappeared back into the bay, they took his fears with them.

He watched as older boys on large wooden boards paddled hard into the swell, which grew bigger and bigger. He loved when they dropped into the waves, riding them like seals at play. When they finished playing in the ocean, they charged out of the cold water, carrying their boards under their arms. Their faces looked icy, and they could barely crack a smile, but they always took the time to stop by the youngster and mess up his hair. They knew better than to talk to him, but like the ocean, they too, watched over little James.

The Plunge housed the second-largest heated, saltwater bath-house in the country. James' mother walked by the one and only lifeguard, Skip Littlefield.

"Late again—I know, I know, little James. Did you leave him on the beach?"

"Yes," his mother said, hanging her head.

"You're just going to have to figure something else out. Can't your mother watch over him?"

"No; it's a long story."

Truth was, her mother was diagnosed with schizophrenia. She started to show signs of the disease in her early twenties, with dramatic mood swings; her perception swung like a pendulum from childlike to paranoid, with frequent panic attacks. She couldn't be trusted with little James.

"He just up and ran out on you, didn't he?" Skip said, referring to James' father.

She couldn't hold back the tears. She felt embarrassed, but they came down hard and fast.

"Pull yourself together and get to work," Skip said. Then he whispered: "I won't tell a soul."

She put on a fake smile and yelled, "Thank you, Mr. Littlefield!"

Just then, she bumped into Malio Rappalino as he broke her fall.

"Woah, woah, woah—slow down there, muffin, or someone's going to get hurt."

She blushed and kept walking. Malio walked over to Littlefield.

"Hello, Littlefield!"

"Malio Rapallino! How's it going?"

Malio shrugged. "You haven't heard?"

"Heard what?" Skip replied. "I'm here from nine in the morning until ten o'clock every night, and that's seven days, to boot!"

Some kids were playing rough, dunking each other and screaming. Skip yelled over to them. "Hey! Cut it out!"

The kids looked over at Skip and Malio and scattered.

"I went to college for this?" Skip said. "I'm making a hundred and twenty dollars a month, and I don't have five minutes to spend a nickel of it! The only thing I know about is right here, or in my dreams."

Malio couldn't wait another minute to tell him the good news.

"The Miss California Pageant is coming to town—and you're not dreaming!"

A pretty young woman walked by and smiled as she heard the news. Both guys stopped, mesmerized by her appearance. She was tall and leggy with long, blond hair; usually women didn't wear their hair down, but this one did. Her teeth were white, and her skin practically glowed.

"I didn't know there was such a thing of beauty until now," Skip mumbled. "She looks like she just crawled out of her knickers."

"For Pete's sake! Did you hear what I said about the pageant? The first Miss California pageant, right here in Santa Cruz, California!"

"Did your family put this together?" Skip asked.

Malio chuckled. "Of course not! After all, we can't do everything!"

Skip let out a long sigh. It had been a long time coming for something like this to happen in Santa Cruz.

"Oh, Malio, this is the greatest thing that ever happened to me."

Malio laughed. "You're telling me?"

Ernest Odda, the reporter, walked up.

"Good afternoon, gentlemen. Nothing like taking a dip in the ocean, especially when it's a pool!"

Just then the emergency alarm went off.

"That's the river alarm! Someone's in trouble!" Skip shouted. He grabbed Malio by the shoulders.

"Can you watch the pool?"

Malio jumped in the lifeguard chair.

"I was born for this. Go get 'em!"

As Skip ran off, Malio comforted the patrons, particularly the female ones.

"It's going to be all right, ladies."

Skip ran outside and Odda followed, bare feet and all. He pulled out his little pad and pen as he chased after Skip.

Outside of The Plunge, Skip jumped on his bicycle and rode to the bridge that crossed over the San Lorenzo River. Odda followed as fast as he could behind him. Skip encountered a frenzy of people pointing to an old fisherman drowning. Skip jumped off of the bridge and into the shallow water below. The fisherman thrashed and gasped as his head slipped in and out of the water.

Skip reached out for him and dragged him safely to shore. Odda interviewed the witnesses. It was just another day at the office for Skip Littlefield and Ernest Odda.

And for little James, as well.

That night, the stars shone and the full moon hung over Cowell's Beach. Little James was half-asleep, curled up in a little ball to keep warm in the cold sand when his mother came to get him.

"Come on, James, my sweet little baby; let's go home."

She picked her little boy up. He wrapped his arms and legs around her body as tightly as he could as she labored through the thick sand.

"It's okay, Mommy. I love you."

Blinded by a light, a beach bird flew by and swooped down on them. His mother dropped James and screamed and thrashed her head around to shake off the bird, which got momentarily caught in her hair. The bird broke free, shrieking as it flew away. James sat crying on the ground. Trembling and out of breath, his mother picked him back up and walked home.

Later that night, a small fire started at the casino. Within hours, the entire place burnt to the ground.

The next morning, Fred stood in front of the smoldering site, wearing only his robe and slippers. Firefighters tried to comfort him, but he was beaten down and exhausted. He knew the arson had something to do with the letters he had received and possibly the mysterious person who yelled out to him at The Plunge only one day before. He stood there, covered in ash, just gazing. He understood the one thing that trumped him in strength, and it was fire. It had taken everything he knew and loved away from him before.

The smell of the salty wet morning air and the smoke made him sick. He thought about the time the Swanson house burned down. He felt the powerlessness of losing everything he owned. He wondered whether the fire was telling him to surrender, or whether he was still right to bring business to Santa Cruz with the casino. He didn't understand people who didn't want to better their lives through corporate growth. He didn't understand why someone might not like him—he wondered whether it was a personal assault or plain misfortune.

He couldn't shake his uneasiness off. As a wave of nausea hit him, he ran to the side of the street, held his stomach, and bent over. But nothing came out. Surely, this ranked as the worst day of his life. He pulled himself together and walked back to the men who worked all night trying to save the establishment.

"I will continue on with my planned summer schedule with no interruptions," he said to the firefighters. "Gentlemen: Thank you very much." Then he climbed up on his horse and rode away in dismay.

FORTY-ONE

Not long afterward, things returned to normal—at least as normal as it gets in Santa Cruz. Agnes worked on recovering from the loss of her mother, but she was shy and didn't go out much. Neighbors worried about her and wondered how she lived with her rich stepfather—or how he lived with her, with her breathtaking beauty. All of the young gents in town wanted to be with Agnes.

And everyone wanted an invitation to visit her house. Her family had the best parties in town. At New Year's Eve, in particular, it was "the place to be" if you were "a somebody." They hosted parties where women dressed in ornate ball gowns; they entertained guests with magic shows, musicals, midnight suppers, and firework displays. They even played the first moving picture in Santa Cruz in their home.

The Major's close friends all accepted invitations to the Villa, including popular politicians such as Theodore Roosevelt and Roosevelt's nephew, Thomas, as well as Con Edison.

One night, as a band marched down the street on Beach Hill, Agnes peeked her head out of a window from the eleven-thousand-square-foot Victorian Villa that her mother and the Major had designed. No one ever knew when she would go out, or when she would sit quietly in The Golden Gate Villa. She had been engaged to Sam Rucker, whom she had been seeing as far back as 1893, but no one knew why they never married. After attending parties night after night, Agnes would devoutly attend Mass every morning at the Holy Cross Catholic Church. She would arrive in a gleaming phaeton pulled by a jet-black horse. As one of the band members saw her, he nudged his friend. She moved quickly out of sight, hiding behind the thick velvet curtain.

Although the casino had burned down, Fred already had erected a massive white tent over the property with a banner reading: "Republican State Convention." Agnes could see it from the veranda upstairs. A few men sat in carved mahogany settees located in the parlor at the MacDonald mansion. Some gazed up at the high ceilings, which showcased gold-plated chandeliers adorned by plaster rosettes. Others remained silent as they relaxed in Spanish feathered stuffed armchairs situated in front of the intricately carved wooden and mirrored mantel next to the full-service bar. The Major had instructed his architect to "spare no expense in making the Golden Gate Villa the showplace of Santa Cruz." He named the house after his very profitable Golden Gate Mining Company. The home featured a room wallpapered with elephant hides, personally given to him from his dear friend and hunting buddy, Teddy Roosevelt. The Major surrounded his fortress with stone walls, handcrafted by Italian masons.

As the men sat around an old Gothic wooden table, one man laid down $14,000. His name was William F. Herrin: Chief Legal Counsel and Broker of the Southern Pacific Railroad.

"That should be sufficient."

Abraham Ruef, a Republican and political boss from San Francisco, scooped up the money and stuffed it in his pocket.

"That will be enough to cover most of the expenses," he said with a greedy smile.

"I should say so," Herrin replied, somewhat paranoid because he knew what he was doing was wrong.

"I've got a train to catch."

"No—stay for dinner," MacDonald said.

"I don't think that would be a very good idea," Herrin said. His eyes appeared cold and black, like hollowed out caves leading to nowhere. It almost gave the Major the shivers. Almost. It takes one to know one, and they were two peas in a pod. As a young man, the Major had served on the police force in Newark, New Jersey, and served in the Union Army, becoming an engineer on the Union Pacific Railroad. He earned a reputation as a six-gun stagecoach driver throughout the Wild West and served as city deputy to Marshall Bat Masterson, who called him "one of the quickest men on the frontier." He was famous for being one of the few men to challenge Wyatt Earp publicly and live to tell the tale. Nothing jolted him.

The longer he could chum with his influential buddies, the better, in his opinion. He mastered the party as a grand scheme, a power trip in which he intended to gather all the power possible. He enjoyed the thrill of the hunt—the chase and ultimate "kill." What he couldn't obtain on his own, he stole, including his daughter, Agnes.

Meanwhile, Fred was downtown when he found an old, drunk Indian lying in the street. He felt slightly embarrassed when the scene triggered an idea for promoting Santa Cruz. "Hey, how would you like free whiskey for the next week? On me, of course!" he asked. The Indian looked up with a crooked smile that curved a little downward on one side. Fred had leaned over to help the man up, when Herrin bumped into him. "Why, hello, Mr. Herrin!" Herrin didn't turn around. He kept walking, hoping no one in town would recognize him.

Later that day, Fred and the Indian sat at the Santa Cruz Hotel. He had dressed the Indian up in a tuxedo and propped him up in a chair in front of the hotel. A photographer took his picture.

Fred exclaimed excitedly, "Oh, that is just beautiful!"

It became a famous tourism poster for Santa Cruz, reading: "Come to Santa Cruz, Where There Are Rich Indians Who Live to Be a Hundred Years Old."

FORTY-TWO

Rowanna felt tired again, but she couldn't stop looking at the photos. It was like reliving the past, and it was better than any class she had ever taken. She wondered why Santa Cruz intrigued her so much.

She took out a photo of Major MacDonald and a group of men perched behind a salon setting. Over at the MacDonald mansion, it was business as usual. Five men in the parlor—the Major, Rueff, and James Gillet, the new governor (paid for by Herrin) posed for the camera shot, along with two others.

Right around that time, President Theodore Roosevelt had caught wind of the controversial issues going on at his close friend's Golden Gate Villa.

Roosevelt picked up the phone.

"It's me, Teddy," he said. "I want a full investigation on Abraham Rueff and all of his associates in San Francisco. Oh, and don't forget MacDonald down in Santa Cruz. I have had enough of these wise guys."

Not too long afterward, *The Sentinel* announced the scandal at the MacDonald home on its front page: The politicians had been bought at the Republican Convention in 1906 in Santa Cruz. As MacDonald read the morning headlines, he was mortified. Exactly one year later, he tried to withdraw money from the bank, only to discover his financial fate had turned into a disaster with zero chance of reconciliation.

His banker and good friend William Jeter told him, "I am sorry, Major; there's nothing I can do."

"How can this be!" MacDonald demanded, pounding his fist on the desk.

Jeter reminded him of all of his assets, which, once liquidated, would surely take care of his expenses until the end.

On the morning of November 16, 1907, Agnes attended a Mass at the Holy Cross Church in memory of her mother, who had died on that date exactly two years before. When she returned home, she walked upstairs to her bedroom in the tower to take a nap. The Major had watched her go into her bedroom, so he sent the maid on a errand and snuck into her room as usual, but only this time, he put a 44 caliber pistol to her temple and shot her in the head. He then called Jeter and told him he must come to the house at once. Jeter declined, stating he would be there when he could. That's when the Major confessed to killing Agnes, saying he was going to kill himself next.

True to his word, he swallowed a fatal dose of potassium cyanide, but he did not take his last breath until his friends arrived. It took Agnes nearly seven hours to die from the gunshot.

In his last words, MacDonald wrote: "I love her so, and so I take her with me." After private services at the villa, Sam Rucker accompanied the bodies to New Jersey, to bury them at the church where the Major had married years before.

But one body remnant remained: a hair that MacDonald had placed inside the twelve-by-nine-foot stained glass image of Agnes, depicting her reaching up to pick an apple-blossomed branch. The picture remains in the house to this day.

FORTY-THREE

Dressed in summer suits, Swanson staged a promotional parade down Pacific Avenue to promote the new casino, the Plunge, and the new hotel, Casa Del Rey. Marching down the street included a twenty-two-piece band, the Army from San Francisco and jugglers, handing out advertising materials, including banner carriers, balloon carriers, toy canes, snappers saying, "Never a Dull Moment," and matchboxes. The materials fell into the hands of residents from Chico to Los Angeles, and as far out east as Nevada.

Swanson and Emma waved to the crowds as they rode in a horse-drawn coach. Emma held a fake smile on her face as she talked to Fred out of the side of her mouth.

"I don't see why you have to be gone so long."

"Oh, don't be silly, my little daffodil," Fred said, in his usual upbeat manner.

"I get so lonely without you. I wish it was like it used to be when you watched me for hours playing the piano, staring lovingly into my eyes."

"Why do we have to go through this every year?" Fred asked. "If I'm not out there promoting, no one will know about us. It's my job."

Emma still had a phony pasted smile on her face.

"What about me? What about us?"

"I'll be back in no time," Fred said, kissing her on the cheek. The carriage strayed from the parade and pulled up to a train, which was about to depart. Emma tried to keep a positive attitude, but her heart sank as she watched him leave again.

"Good-bye!"

"Not good-bye—never good-bye, my darling," Fred shouted, as each blew a kiss to the other.

When Fred returned, Emma saw how the tour had paid off. She stood on the red carpet with Fred, genuinely laughing as cameras and reporters crammed to catch a glimpse of them. So many people swarmed the area; it would have looked like an anthill from a plane. People stood on the pier, near the roller coaster, and on the *Balboa* boat in the bay.

FORTY-FOUR

Rowanna still held a couple of photos in her hand, and she couldn't wait to jump into the next scene. She got up and made herself another cup of tea, only this time she seeped black tea to keep her tired eyes awake and alert.

Then she picked up the next photo.

In April 1927, the Civic Center was decked out for an election. Fred Swanson was now sixty-five years old and running for mayor. He stood behind one podium, while his main opponent, Thomas Bartley, stood behind another. C.W. Balzari, the third opponent, stood next to the two proudly: It was a tight race. Emma stood behind Fred with their daughter Pearl.

"And I would have no political promises and no selected advisory committee, like my opponents do," Swanson said. "My wish is to have the entire populace of Santa Cruz as my advisors!"

The crowd went crazy. The announcer began to deliver the vote counts.

"Balzari has 509 votes."

Balzari looked down.

"Bartley has 1,147 votes."

Bartley tightened his lips and grit his teeth.

"And Swanson has 2,360 votes!"

The announcer held out his arms and said, "Ladies and gentle-men, I would like to introduce to you, Mayor Swanson!"

The crowd roared. Thousands of red, white, and blue balloons floated skyward as a band began to play.

Later inside the Civic Center, Fred and Emma talked to the people standing in line. The district attorney, Stanford Smith, walked up and congratulated Fred.

"Thank you. Have you met my lovely wife?" Fred asked.

"No, I haven't had the pleasure."

Smith nodded at her respectfully. Fred called over Ernest Odda, who was listening to one of the losers, Thomas Bartley, speak.

"I would like an explanation from Swanton on what his plans are to clean up this town," Bartley yelled out. "What about the prohibition?"

Odda scurried over to Swanton for his reply. The room grew quiet.

"It's funny you should mention that, Bartley. Thank you. Ernest, make sure you get all of this down. I want everyone to remember what I am about to say in regards to Bartley's question."

Ernest listened as a photographer snapped several photos of Swanson, who now stood next to Smith.

"Smith, I am asking you to uphold the anti-liquor laws of the nation. You will get full backing from the Santa Cruz Police Department."

"Very well then, Swanson," Smith said with enthusiasm.

FORTY-FIVE

Nothing ever seemed normal in classroom number nine, and the next day was no different.

"Today, we are going to dip a little into a day and the life of the Italians," Rowanna told the class. "Giliano is writing a lengthy report about Prohibition in the 1920s and what it might have been like for his Italian relatives when they were in charge of a few things here. He is going to be a writer some day. Here's an excerpt from the piece he is working on."

Giliano reluctantly stood up in front of the class.

"Uuuhh…"

He pushed his thick glasses higher up the bridge of his nose.

"I am starting in the middle because I am putting the entire story together in pieces. I don't have the beginning written yet, uuhh…"

"Fine, fine, just read it," Rowanna said, gently nudging him.

Giliano began to read the most intimate piece he had ever written. He had grown up in a loud and proud Italian family, which had run a lucrative business for many, many years on the waterfront of Santa Cruz.

"Later on that night, Malio was in a gambling parlor," Giliano began reading. "There were several men at the tables gambling. Prostitutes surrounded the tables. Everyone was drunk. It was against the law for the Chinese to own real property. Malio's Italian family, the Rapallinos, owned and operated all of the gambling and opium dens in Chinatown."

Randy and Eric looked at each other with raised eyebrows.

Giliano could feel the thick air as he sucked it in. His throat started to close up, and he coughed. The whole class stared in disbelief, trying to process the fact that Giliano Lombardi, of all the kids, had it in him to write such a thing. The content coming from his mouth was hardly predictable.

"Nothing surprises me anymore," Holly mumbled. "I think now I can honestly say I have seen it all."

Giliano continued.

"In the back of the establishment, a wealthy, obese Chinese man sat in a small room. Malio walked up to him: 'Hello, hello. Got something for me, my friend?'

"The fat man got up, gave Malio a hug, and handed a bag over to him.

"'Kisses to the Mrs.,' Malio said as he took the bag.

"The Chinaman laughed and gave him a wink. 'You got it.'

"Malio headed to the C. Rapallino Fishing Corporation, located on the municipal wharf, where he met Conttardo I and Conttardo II. Conttardo I sat in a wheelchair in front of stacks of crates of alcohol. There were also stacks of money on a table in front of them. Conttardo I spoke in a heavy, slow Italian accent.

"'We are going to be unloading all night. We got more deliveries coming in at 3 a.m. In the meantime, Wong's having a little problem downtown collecting from a couple of his visitors. I need you to round up the boys and take care of business.'

"'When are these guys going to learn?' Conttardo II asked.

"Malio shook his head in agreement as they headed out the door.

"'Oh, and boys,' Conttardo I added, 'tell Wong hello for me.'

"A short while later, Malio, Conttardo II, Tisto, Babe, and Risho entered into the gambling parlor. It was popular, noisy, and packed with smoke, alcohol, and gambling tables. As soon as the patrons saw the men enter, they became quiet. The Italians spread out and looked around. Several businessmen occupied the adjoining room, called the opium den.

"Malio walked up to a table, and his cousins followed. It was already occupied, but the men sitting there immediately got up and left. Everyone sat down except for Conttardo. Wong nodded over to the troublemakers. Conttardo circled around the two men, leaning over them and sniffing, like a wolf. They had entered the parlor to party, but Conttardo's behavior made them stiffen.

"'I smell whiskey. Tisto, do you smell whiskey?'

"Tisto walked over to the table and sniffed the men.

"'Oh, yeah, that's whiskey, all right.'

"'Whiskey's illegal in the United States,' Conttardo II said. 'Did you know that?'

"'Well, yeah, but we're here in Santa Cruz,' the men, who were tourists, replied.

"'Do you have a point?' Conttardo asked, angrily.

"'Everyone knows it's bootlegger's paradise here,' they said.

"Without taking his eyes off of them, Conttardo signaled for Tisto to speak.

"'Lesson number one,' Tisto said. 'If you can't afford to pay, then you can't play. Didn't your mother teach you that?'

"He punched one of them. The tourist cried out. He held his bleeding lip to stop the flow.

"'Oh, please,' the tourist said, referring to the Chinese running the shop, 'they are just a bunch of celestials! They don't deserve the money! Who cares?'

"Babe walked over. Still holding his mouth, the guy with the busted lip got up from the table and backed up slowly. Babe grabbed his shirt and slapped him hard across the face. The tourist panicked, whining: 'Oh no, no please.' His friend got up from the table, pushed up his spectacles, and said, 'Can't we settle this properly?'

"Malio ripped the glasses off of his face. 'You see; that's lesson number two. If this was settled properly, then we wouldn't have to be here, now would we Risho?'

"'That's what seems to be the problem,' Risho replied.

"'You guys come here from out of town, thinking you're going to take whatever you want and leave. I am sick and tired of having to get up in the middle of the night, night after night, to school stupid, greedy men like you.'

"Risho whacked the guy across his knees with a pole."

"Whoa!" yelled Randy from the back of the classroom, laughing aloud.

Giliano was so engrossed in his storytelling—as if he lived it himself—he didn't flinch when Randy yelled out. He just kept going.

"With his friend on the floor, holding his knees in pain, the first guy was shaking in his pants.

"'Who are you guys?'

"'That's lesson number three: We're the enforcers,' Babe said, holding up his hands. 'And personally, I don't like to get my hands dirty.'

"Suddenly, the tourists heard Indian drumming. Then they saw an Indian ghost standing right behind Conttardo and heard the loud Pogonip scream—half-human, half-animal. His long black hair flew around his head, and his red eyes glared.

"'What was that?' one of the tourists shouted. The other hid his face.

"'What are you looking at?' Tisto yelled.

"'You had your chance to do the right thing,' Risho said, backing up Tisto.

"'Since we had to leave our warm, cozy, homes to set you losers straight, you're going to give us all of your money—all of it! Then you are going to leave town tonight, and if you don't...' Risho's eyes flashed red, 'you are going to wake up in about ten pieces on the bottom of the bay.'

"The tourists pulled their pockets inside out and dumped everything they had onto the floor. They had more than what they owed to Wong and the establishment. The two men backed up slowly with their hands up in the air, then stumbled out the door.

"'Boys, looks like our business is finished here,' Conttardo said, turning to the others in the parlor, 'Gentlemen: As you were.'

"They returned to the municipal pier at three in the morning right on time while the bootlegger was throwing his last crate of alcohol off the boat and onto the dock. Babe handed him a wad of cash and turned and walked away. The bootlegger said, 'Hey! How do I know it's all here?'

"Without turning around, Babe said, 'You can count, can't ya?'

"'I'll be back next month,' the bootlegger whispered through the thick fog.

"Babe mumbled to himself, 'Yeah, yeah, yeah—I won't hold my breath.'"

Giliano returned to his normal speaking voice to teach his fellow students about Prohibition.

"Prohibition lasted from 1920 to 1933 and was known as The Noble Experiment. The results of the experiment were clear: innocent people suffered; organized crime grew into an empire; the police, courts, and politicians became increasingly corrupt; disrespect for the law grew; and the per capita consumption of the prohibited substance—alcohol—increased dramatically every year. In fact, alcohol use never returned to its pre-1920 levels. People wanted alcohol, and people like the Rapallinos were there to give the people what they needed. The boats would pull up to the pier at night under the pretense of filling up their tanks with gas, and people would load their decks with crates of every kind of alcohol they could get their hands on."

Giliano stopped and hurried back to his seat without looking around.

"Wow, Giliano. You wrote all of that yourself?" Ms. Rowanna asked.

"Yes," replied Giliano.

"Are you finished?"

"Well, I do have this other piece, but it doesn't fit in exactly to what I was just reading."

"Would you like to read it anyway?" Ms. Rowanna asked.

"Only if I can do it sitting down from here," Giliano replied.

"Class, do you want to hear some more?"

The students egged Giliano on as he blushed and started to read again.

FORTY-SIX

"There was a parade for the Miss California Pageant," Giliano began. "The whole town showed up. Some of the contestants rode in luxury floats, while others walked. They all wore brightly colored banners as they strutted down the street, waving gracefully. The Ku Klux Klan led the parade, and though many people opposed their presence, no one dared speak against them. People of color hid their faces in fear or shame as the K.K.K. traveled proudly past the crowd.

"The Rapallino cousins stood up on a rooftop for the best view. As they passed around a bottle, each took a generous swig.

"Before they saw the K.K.K., Babe exclaimed, 'Oh this is going to be great!'

"'This is it,' Risho said. 'The moment we've all been waiting for!'

"Malio saw them first.

"'What is that? I can't even see their faces. What's going on with the sheets over the heads? Is it some kind of joke? Tisto—Do you know?'

"'The K.K.K.,' Tisto said.

"'I know who they are! What are they doing here?' Malio asked angrily. 'Oh, that's it! That's it! I'm outa here!'

"It was a reminder that the Rapallinos didn't hold all of the power in Santa Cruz. There were other powers at large as well. And everyone held a place in the pecking order. The Italians were prime targets for the Ku Klux Klan; the white-cloaked group considered Italians dirty, greasy minorities.

"Babe was the last to leave the rooftop. He stopped to look one last time before turning around to leave. He stared long and hard at one of the K.K.K. members. He looked so intensely, he could see right through the hooded disguise.

"He could hear light Indian drumming and the sound of a rattlesnake shaker hissing. He looked around to see where it originated from, and then looked back at one of the hooded impostors. The hooded man stopped and stared up at Babe as if he knew him.

"The Pogonip ghost screamed, and the hooded man held his ears and stumbled away.

"Later, up on a grassy hilltop not far away, the white-hooded men stood around a fire, chanting quietly at first and then growing louder and louder. Someone lit a torch, and the fire spread to thirteen crosses. They burned thirteen crosses that night in the name of the white race of man and in the name of the Ku Klux Klan. They represented just a small portion of the five-million Ku Klux Klan members in America in the mid-1920s."

Giliano peeked up at his classmates to see whether they were still interested. All eyes were on him so he ventured to go on.

"Here's my last piece that I am tying into the story.

"The Italians ruled the waterfront. They owned three restaurants, two coffeehouses, a fuel station, three speedboats, and a half-a-dozen fishing boats. What really completed the family was their reputation as hard workers and their businesses relating directly to the fishing industry. The other businesses fed off of that. They played Italian music in the Sports Fishers Coffee Shop on the municipal pier.

"One day, after the parade, Conttardo Peter Rapallino I sat with Conttardo II and Swanson at their family-owned and operated restaurant.

"'Let Wong know they'll be moving in next week,' Swanson said. 'It has to be done. I am very sorry. It won't happen again.'

"A beautiful woman walked up. Her name was Lucky Lucy.

"'Anything else I can get you, Mr. Swanson?'

"'I'm good to go; thank you, Lucky.'

"She asked Conttardo, 'How about you boys? Anything else?'

"'We're good, darling,' Contarrado said. 'Thank you.'

"Not too long after, the officials surrounded Wong's packed gambling parlor and opium den. They burst through the door into a room where loud music played and prostitutes danced on the tables while men gambled and drank.

"'Everyone down!' the officials said, shooting their guns into the air.

"Wong was not surprised.

"Some men tried to run away, only to be beaten to a pulp and dragged off to jail. That night was the beginning of the end of the illegal use of drugs and alcohol in Chinatown.

"And that's the end of my story, for now," Giliano said just as the bell rang.

Rowanna approached him as many of the students did, with questions.

"The curse. You put the curse in the story. That is the making of a very interesting book—please turn your report into a book," Rowanna said. "I want to take a look at it when it is done. I may know someone who can help you with it."

"Why don't you just write about the whole dang history of the curse of Santa Cruz? That would make for a perfect story," Viper said as he stormed out of the room. "This class is crazy! You are all crazy!"

Randy patted Giliano on the back. "Good job, Ragu. That was mind-bending—was that for real?"

"Is he patronizing me?" Giliano asked Howard.

"Giliano, the whole world isn't out to get us," Howard said. "Leave some room for the good things to get in, too."

"Look, Giliano; we should get together," Eric said. "My relatives and yours, well, they were friends. They all knew each other. Weird or what? Let's work together."

"How?" asked Giliano. "I am already writing it."

"If you need any help or want some information, just let me know," Eric said.

"Looks to me like you are all in this together," Rowanna said.

"Maybe you are right," Giliano replied. "Maybe."

He still wasn't sure whether he could trust Eric, but he wanted to.

"Eric, can you please wait?" Rowanna asked. "I need a minute with you."

"Sure."

As the class filed out, she handed Eric his photos.

"You forgot these yesterday. I took them home last night and spent the entire evening looking at them. I am actually quite exhausted—barely slept a wink. This one was the saddest."

She pulled out a photo dated September 1940. It depicted Fred Swanson's funeral.

As Rowanna drifted off into a trance, Eric wondered what was going on. She even began to narrate the scene, in a deeper voice, like a man's.

"Hundreds of people swarmed the Holy Cross Church to pay their respects and say good-bye. Emma, your great-grandmother, spoke at the service about her beloved husband."

Rowanna's voice changed again, as if she were channeling Emma's spirit.

"'We had a good solid marriage. We raised a wonderful daughter.'"

The tears welled up as she looked over at Pearl, and tears welled up in Rowanna's eyes as well.

"'Truth is, I could never hold a candle to Santa Cruz. Fred left many times in hopes of a better future for the business and our family. But he always came back to her: Santa Cruz. Many times, we faced opposition in our town, and not only did it frighten me, but also, it saddened poor Fred. He left no stone unturned. He expanded our small lumber city into a booming beach city. I would like to thank the people of Santa Cruz for electing my husband mayor three terms in a row. And for all of the support we have received over the years.'

"Emma began to weep.

"'Not good-bye, my darling. Never good-bye.'"

As Emma collapsed from the podium and Pearl escorted her mother away—so, too, did Rowanna almost collapse, but Eric caught her. Gaining her footing, Rowanna's voice deepened, much like a man's again.

"Sadly, she never recovered from the loss of her husband."

Tearfully, Rowanna snapped out of it and handed the photos back to Eric.

"I'm sorry. I am very sensitive," Rowanna said. "Please excuse me."

"It's all right, but I gotta go now," Eric said, feeling uncomfortable not just with Rowanna's outburst, but also with how everyone around him acted so strange lately.

FORTY-SEVEN

The Bates Motel, from the movie *Psycho*, still stood at 80 Front Street in Santa Cruz. Randy and Eric were standing smack in the middle of the creepy structure that had inspired one of the most successful horror films in Hollywood's history. Randy lit a joint and offered some to Eric.

"You know I hate that shit, man," Eric said.

"Just double-checking," said Randy.

"I'll never understand why people put that in their system," Eric said.

"Yeah, I guess some habits die hard," Randy said, turning away and extinguishing the joint.

"I'm sorry, dude," Randy said.

"I'm here for you no matter what." Eric gave him a hard pat on the back.

"It's okay; I'm over it anyway," Randy said.

The boys hesitated about entering the building, but they didn't want to look like cowards in front of Viper, who, little did they know, was standing behind them and then suddenly disappeared.

"You know this is the real *Psycho* house, right?" Eric said. "The one that inspired Alfred Hitchcock's movie *Psycho*. Hitchcock lived here when he created his two most famous movies. There was something about Santa Cruz that inspired him. *The Birds* was about something that really happened here too."

"Wow," said Randy, looking around with a bead of sweat rolling down his forehead. "That's nice to know. Thanks for sharing."

They walked up what seemed to be a hundred stairs to the Gothic doorway and knocked hard. No one answered, so they slowly crept in. The tall skinny door creaked as they pushed through it. They slipped into a golden-lit room with a fire glowing in the fireplace. Eric couldn't help but notice the high ceilings and the faded paint, which peeled and curled around the corners of the doorways. The old, soft wooden floors felt like they could fall through at any given time.

Eric thought it peculiar that no one was around, while Randy's palms started to sweat.

"What the hell? Is someone screwing with us?" Randy asked, looking at the fire. Eric sat down by the fire on a little couch covered by a floral wrap.

"This sure is comfy," Eric said.

"So what's the story here?" Randy asked, against his better judgment.

"Are you sure you want to hear about it right now?"

"Why not? I'm not even scared," Randy said, trying to ignore his sweaty palms. Randy surveyed the room and swung his leg over the top of the couch.

"The Bates Mansion in *Psycho*—this place we are in now—was directly copied from this very structure right here on Front Street. And this actual property has been plagued since the day it was built. No one ever owned it for very long; people sold it over and over. Some say it used to be a bar and a haven for prostitution at some point.

"Later, local drug addicts squatted here. Many say the property is haunted. Plus, the house is built on a sacred Indian burial ground. All of the people who have lived here experienced bad luck because of the sacred dirt it was built on. In fact, much of Santa Cruz was developed on Indian burial grounds, but no one knows exactly when they'll find the sacred sites, until they start digging. When developers find bones, the fight is over the land to determine if it should be considered 'sacred' and left alone or not. They don't see it as a cry out from the ancestral indigenous people and the wrongful taking of their people and their land. For them, it's just another notch in their belts."

By this time, Randy crowded Eric, almost hugging him for comfort.

"Dude! Get off me!" Eric said.

FORTY-EIGHT

Rowanna stood on her deck, trying to catch her breath. Too much was happening, too quickly, for her to maintain a grip on reality. The sun had set and she was experiencing unwanted visions she couldn't shake off.

"No, no please stop," she asked no one in particular, but it didn't change anything.

She found herself back at the MacDonald Mansion as lightning, and then thunder, struck. The Pogonip ghost screeched like fingers on a blackboard. She held her hands over her ears to try to block it out.

Then she had another flashback.

It was a sunny afternoon. Agnes was taking a nap in the parlor. MacDonald came in with a gun and shot her in the head and then screamed. His scream turned into the Pogonip screech, and then he turned into the ghost. MacDonald rushed to the kitchen and drank a bottle of cyanide. Then he ran down Third Street toward Cliff Street. He stopped at 417 Cliff Street, in front of a huge, white Victorian home. His neighbor was clipping bushes in the garden.

The half-demon, half-human, ghostly figure of MacDonald cried out: "I just shot Agnes! I just shot her dead!"

The confession terrified the neighbor, who ran to his door for cover. MacDonald, in a controlled fury, said, "Oh, no, no, no, no—

don't try anything stupid. It's too late for me anyway. Cyanide—just polished off the bottle. I'll be gone in...in...in..."

He loudly groaned and seemingly dropped dead. The neighbor crept back over to look at him, holding his large clippers in hand, just in case.

Rowanna suddenly was transported back into the present moment. The Pogonip ghost began talking to her as her cats scratched at the screen door, trying to reach her.

"Number nine, number nine, calling number nine! Hello, gorgeous! Did it hurt?" the ghost whispered.

"What?"

"When you fell down from heaven?" The ghost roared with laughter.

She lost her strength and fell into the corner of the deck. Visions of being abducted by a stalker in the 1970s when she was a reporter flooded her. She met a man. They were both drinking in a bar on the municipal pier. He was very attractive and told her everything she wanted to hear. She was beautiful, funny, and talented. He had been watching her for weeks on the local news station and became completely obsessed and started covertly stalking her.

He asked her to think of something—anything—and then write it down and don't show it to him or tell him what it was. Then he replied back to her exactly what she wrote. She was astounded: There was no way he could know. She made him do it over and over, and then asked him to do it with some other people at the bar. Time and time again, he described, in explicit detail, what they were thinking.

"Are you a clairvoyant?" she asked.

"No, I am the devil."

Blurry-eyed and drunk out of her mind, Rowanna couldn't think or see clearly and began to laugh aloud.

"I love a man with a sense of humor," she said as she dabbed her eyes with a cocktail napkin, so as not to smear her mascara.

She asked him to walk to the end of the pier and back, and then they decided to walk to town for another drink. But they never made it there. On the way up the hill, he began to tell her the history of the old 40 Front Street property. Then he led her into the back of the property and tried to kiss her, but she resisted. This enraged him, and he pulled out duct tape and tied her up. Apparently, he had planned it all along.

She tried to scream, but he grabbed her face and squeezed her mouth shut with his big hands until he could tape her mouth shut. He threw her on the ground and pulled out a pair of pantyhose, tying them around her neck tightly. Then he raped her repeatedly, and when he was done, he pounded her head several times into the ground until she quit breathing.

Before he vacated the scene, he cut the pantyhose from her neck and pulled one legging up and over his head to disguise himself as he fled. While he scrambled out from the bushes, a passerby spotted him and yelled out, "Hey! What are you doing? Do you need help?"

But the murderous man ran away. No one ever found out his true identity—not even Rowanna.

She curled up in a little ball as the visions kept coming. The tormenting entity appeared again.

"Do you remember me now? It was me. I left you for dead. But you survived. I am the dark. I am every fear you ever had. I am the misery that consumes life and every tear that is shed. I am you, and you can't get rid of me—not ever. I will prevail. You are mine. This world is mine."

Boom. She was back in the 1930s at the Casino Ballroom. A beautiful blonde woman sat on the stage, wearing a crown. It was her—over eighty years ago. She was the first winner of the Miss California pageant. People danced to music and drank up a storm. The place was packed and out of control. In the bay, she could see the *Balboa*, a big gambling boat that little boats shuffled people back and forth to.

Next, she found herself on a grassy mountaintop. It was cold and dark. White-hooded people wearing long white robes stood in a circle around a fire, chanting quietly. She could see their lips were moving through their hoods, but she couldn't hear what they were saying over the cheerful music playing at the waterfront casino. Suddenly, the hooded men broke out of the circle and moved into a straight line to witness the burning of a cross. In the background, behind the cross, the Pogonip ghost's hair flew wildly in the wind. He rode a horse that reared up and out of control. Rowanna turned around and saw dozens of crosses burning throughout the city hills.

In the vast, dark sky, a meteor shower appeared, and she heard the song "Mr. Sandman" play as Eric spoke in a dreamy, ghostly voice.

"When Great-Grandpa Swanson died, three quarters of the town showed up. A lot of people tried to take credit for what he did for us, but I know who he was."

Suddenly, a warm light grew around Rowanna. It got bigger and bigger, and out of it walked her grandmother.

"Rowanna…Rowanna," she whispered.

Rowanna recognized the voice and then saw the figure.

"Rowanna, my darling. My sweet grandbaby. Look at me."

Rowanna felt confused, but then her grandmother's voice became powerful and strong.

"Rowanna, look at me. Look at the light. You have nothing to be afraid of."

"Grandma?"

"Yes, Rowanna, it's me. Now I want you to do something very important. This is all a lie. Forgive him. Forgive him, and release him. Pull the dark in close, and love it until it is diffused into the light. It's the only way out."

"Okay, Grandma. Okay."

With the light swirling around her, Rowanna pulled herself from the deck floor, stumbling at first and then standing tall, as the cats meowed wildly, continuing to tear at the screen door. Facing the demon, she held out her arms and welcomed him into her heart.

"Come to me. I will take you in. We will be together forever."

The demon ghost laughed and said, "Not so easy!"

"Breathe it in and love it," her grandmother said in a stronger voice. "Don't be afraid."

Rowanna stood with her arms spread out, long and wide, and repeated the words: "I forgive you. I forgive you. I forgive you. Come to me; I forgive you."

Slowly, the evil force seeped into her heart and dissolved into the light. She felt a warm, tingling feeling all over, much like that of an electrical vibration shooting through her entire body, unlike anything she had ever felt before. She felt more vibrant, more alive than she had in years. She heard a voice of a woman behind her speaking softly.

"Thank you."

She turned around and saw a cloaked Indian woman, the same one who had passed her by during the birds' incident she covered as a reporter in 1961. The woman still wore her hooded, burgundy velvet cape.

Rowanna approached her and gently pulled the hood back, placing her warm hands over the woman's shoulders. They both bathed in the radiant light surrounding them.

"You now know the touch of divine light that illuminates your soul," the Indian woman said. "You now understand the true meaning of humility and the importance of forgiveness. But please understand, dear sister, one thing: This is not the end. This is a new beginning of what is, what has always been, and what will always be—immeasurable, unchangeable, unconditional love."

She softly cupped her hand around Rowanna's cheek.

"Thank you for giving us the voice to tell our story."

Then she handed Rowanna a letter.

"Read this to as many people as you can."

She snapped her finger.

"You are now awake."

Clear-headed, Rowanna heard a school bell ring. Rowanna woke up in her bed with the cats cuddling at her legs. She knew she hadn't been dreaming, but she couldn't figure out how she ended up in bed—with the cats, no less. Surely she must have been dreaming.

That's when she discovered the letter the Indian woman gave her.

FORTY-NINE

Back at the *Psycho* mansion, shit was hitting the fan. Upstairs in a bedroom, a ghostly prostitute was in bed with a man on top of her when she let out an ear-piercing shriek.

"What was that?" Eric asked.

"I don't know, and I don't want to know!" Randy replied.

Still, the boys couldn't help but investigate. They ran upstairs where the man was abusing her. As they busted through the door, the man turned his face toward them. It was Viper. But he was an old man who immediately vanished into thin air.

Randy and Eric ran back down the stairs and into the living room where they found a satanic ritual going on. People dressed in dark capes held hands in a circle around a sacrificial table stacked with candles. They chanted as a crying little girl awaited her destiny. When Eric and Randy discovered what was going on, they ran to the child; it turned out to be Leslie. Viper ripped his hood off and laughed triumphantly. His eyes were blood red as he spoke.

"I am everywhere: What are you going to do about it?"

He laughed as Randy charged at him.

Randy fought and fought until he almost passed out. His strength was no match for the demon, but it bought Eric time to release Leslie.

Holly ripped the hood off of her head and ran to Randy, pulling him away from Viper and falling into his arms.

"Oh, Randy, I thought you would never get here; I am getting so sick of this satanic crap. Will you please forgive me for being so awful?"

"Forgive you? I've loved you since the first grade," Randy replied.

They embraced and kissed.

"Are you hungry?" Eric asked Leslie.

"Starved."

"How about some Chinese food?" Randy asked, taking Holly by the hand, then joining with the others, hand-in-hand, to fight the evil force attempting to restrain them.

Viper levitated and screamed, "It's not over! It'll never be over!"

As they ran out of the house and walked downtown for food, they began to talk about Viper's past.

"It's like he came out of nowhere," Randy said. "Who are his parents?"

"I have no idea—it's so freaky," Eric said.

"I never met them or was allowed near his house," Holly said. "I don't even know where he lives."

FIFTY

Dusk began approaching as Tim stood outside of the coffeehouse reading the story about what happened in Santa Cruz. With a warm cup of hot chocolate in hand, he leaned up against the wall and read on: "On October 17, 1989, at about 5:04 p.m., earth began to rumble. Located practically on the San Andreas fault line, Santa Cruz rocked and rolled as the earth shook in waves, longer and harder. It was a "big one," an earthquake registering on the Richter Magnitude Scale of 7.1. It lasted fifteen seconds, but the hundreds of aftershocks, including a 5.2 forty-five minutes later, caused old buildings to fall and people to run out of their homes and workplaces. The quake severely damaged the Pacific Garden Mall, and falling debris killed three people, half of the six deaths due to the earthquake in Santa Cruz County.

"The police and fire officials considered the citizens who worked to help their friends escape from the rubble, a nuisance, but the residents continued their efforts in the dark. Police eventually arrested those who refused to stop searching. They found another woman—who could have been saved—dead under a collapsed wall.

"Days later, the harsh police reaction became a political issue, splitting the town up against law officials, causing complete havoc. In the end, thirty-one buildings warranted demolition—seven of which had been listed in the Santa Cruz Historic Building Survey. Both Ford's Department Store and the Santa Cruz Coffee Roasting Company had collapsed upon customers and employees. Two police officers crawled through voids in the debris and found one victim alive and another dead inside the coffee house. Santa Cruz beach lifeguards helped move the victims. The police forced employed dogs to help locate further victims. A woman was found dead inside Ford's.

"Meanwhile, family members, coworkers, and friends held candlelight vigils and prayed outside of the Santa Cruz Roasting Company. In the first few days following the quake, electric power remained out for most Santa Cruz County subscribers, and some areas had no water. Cell phone service remained online, providing a crucial link for rescue workers. Widespread search operations began in order to find victims trapped within fallen structures. Six teams of dogs and their handlers went to work. A number of residential structures sustained damage, with some knocked off of their foundations. Many residents slept outside of their homes, concerned about aftershocks, of which there were fifty-one with magnitudes higher than 3.0 in the following twenty-four hours, plus sixteen more the second day."

"My God," Tim thought. "That would be terrifying." It was one thing he had to be grateful about. He was safe and standing on solid ground—for now—as he savored the last of his hot chocolate and walked toward his car.

FIFTY-ONE

A monarch butterfly landed on an old cypress tree at the lighthouse field, where the Ohlone Indians used to play so long ago. It was a warm and sunny day in October 2003. Just down the street, James Gordy stood in front of the house he was born and raised in, over three quarters of a century before. He slid a bottle out from his pocket and took a swig. A rough-looking biker came out of the house.

"What are you looking at, old man?"

Gordy took another swig.

"This is the oldest standing two-story in town. It used to be a pig farm. You see these hedges? They used to be ten feet tall, and they grew all the way back to Oxford Street. It's where I had my first kiss."

"No shit!" said the biker as he lit a cigarette.

"This was where my grandmother and my mother died," Gordy said. "It all seems like yesterday. My life passed me by in the blink of an eye."

Taking to the bottle had made it worse.

"You want a beer?" the biker asked, inviting him into the backyard. Gordy peeked into the side window; he swore he caught a glimpse of his grandmother looking at him. It took his breath away for a moment. He didn't dare say a word about it to the "tough guy" who now resided there.

"So then what happened?" the biker asked.

"I was a surfer and a smart ass. I got into a lot of trouble. I left for the war and swore I would never come back to this house."

The biker cracked open a beer and handed it to Gordy. Gordy visualized the day he left the house for good, ready to fight in World War II. He was drunk and yelling at his grandmother and his mother. They tried to comfort each other because he scared them. He was intoxicated, belligerent, and violent.

"I don't ever want to see either of you again. I hate both of you. I am never coming back here again. Never!"

"Please don't leave us, James," his mother said, weeping. "You're all we have—we're scared to live alone. Please don't go. We love you."

"That's what I used to tell you when you left me on the beach when I was five years old."

His mother fell to her knees. He looked at his grandmother.

"And where were you? Crazy. That's where."

Gordy walked out the door and slammed it. That was the last time he saw either one of them.

"You get old and realize you made some mistakes," he said.

He took a gulp of his beer and looked up at the bedroom window. He thought he saw his mother's ghost, and he smiled at her as tears began to roll down his face.

"You can only pray you are forgiven for the mistakes you made that you can never take back."

His mother smiled back.

"Damn! That's some heavy shit!" the biker said. "Wanna another beer?"

Gordy shook his head.

"Naa. I have to go now."

"Are you sure?"

"Gotta go; gotta go now," Gordy said, as he wiped his eyes dry.

"Stop by anytime, you hear, old man?"

"Yeah, sure."

FIFTY-TWO

That same day, Eric and Randy drove down to the lane to check the waves. They couldn't believe it: As luck would have it, Gordy was there. Everyone knew and loved Gordy. He was one of the first surfers in Santa Cruz.

Gordy was off in a daze, staring out at the sea and remembering his childhood. It was the first day of school at Almar Park School. Kids ran around as Miss Sarah, the teacher, tried to corral them into the classroom.

"James, please! James! I need everyone to calm down. James, please come here."

Six kids ran over to her.

"I just said James." All six boys said: "I am James."

Miss Sarah was surprised.

"All of you are named James?" Miss Sarah asked in disbelief as she fanned her face. "Oh, my. I need a glass of water."

Once everyone settled down, she gave all of the boys named James a nickname. She arrived at Gordy's desk.

"And what is your middle name, young man?"

"Gordy."

"Gordy what?" she asked.

"It's just Gordy."

She corrected him.

"You answer: 'It's just Gordy, Miss Sarah.' Have I made myself clear?"

"Yes, ma'am," Gordy responded as he sunk into this chair. "I mean, 'Yes, ma'am, Miss Sarah.'"

"Well then, 'Gordy,' it is," she said. "Now, Gordy, where was your mother this morning? I didn't get a chance to meet her."

She wondered why Gordy was so dirty and wondered what kind of mother could send her child to school like that.

Gordy's mother always left early for work and rarely had any money to buy much food. The house didn't have hot water, so he washed himself in the cold, salty ocean. Gordy felt ashamed that he was the only one who didn't have a father. He had no other relatives to help; he relied solely on his mother. His grandmother was completely absent.

As Miss Sarah moved on to another student, she thought to herself, "At least he made it to school."

Later on that day, little James sat on the sand at Cowell's Beach, waiting for his mom to get off work. A surfer walked up to him and said, "Aren't you tired of just watching? Why don't you come and get wet with us?"

"Huh?" said six-year-old James. "Me?"

The surfers laughed. "Yeah, *you!*" the surfer said, chuckling.

"You are going to take *me* out there with *you?*"

"That sounds like the plan—that is if you want to."

"But what about the sharks?"

The surfers laughed even harder.

"We'll tell you what: We won't bother them if they don't bother us. Sound fair?"

"All right!" James said as he jumped up and followed them to the water's edge.

"Hey, little buddy, my name is Darren Steward. What's yours?"

"James," he said, grinning.

"James? Well, James, this here is my friend Wayne Polly."

A few moments later, they jumped into the water and put James on the front of Steward's 75-pound board and paddled out. They rode over the tops of crashing waves. Steward yelled, "Hang on James!"

James held on for the first ride of his life. Soon, they began to catch wave after wave until they couldn't tolerate the cold water any longer. James rode in on his last wave, standing on the front tip section of Steward's board. Wayne was right next to them.

"Go, James! Go, little buddy! You did it!"

They escorted him back to the beach where they found him and wrapped a torn and tattered towel around him. Then they opened an old canteen with warm water in it, let him drink some, and then poured a little bit over his head.

"We'll see you tomorrow. Should be pretty good."

As they walked away, James knew he had found the answer to his loneliness. He felt like there was a God, and it wasn't his mother—it was the ocean. And he wanted to spend his life there, not just looking at it, but in it.

FIFTY-THREE

Gordy let his mind drift back to 1912, when a famous surfer from Hawaii, Duke Kahanamoku, came to town for a visit. It was the same year Duke set an Olympic record in the 100-meter freestyle in Stockholm and won the silver in the 400-meter relay.

When he returned, Duke embarked upon a worldwide campaign to encourage surfing. Surfing had come to Santa Cruz already, but Duke was one of the first Hawaiians to hang ten in the city.

Gordy thought about the earliest surfers from the islands, which legend had it were three Hawaiian princes who tested the waters at the San Lorenzo river mouth in Santa Cruz in 1885.

At the time, Princes David Kawnanakoa, Edward Keli'iahonui and Jonah Khi Kalaniana'ole—nephews of Queen Kapi'olani—were attending St. Matthew's, a military-style boys' school in San Mateo. As teenagers, they constructed their surfboards from California redwoods that weighed up to ninety pounds. At that time, their surfing spirit didn't catch on—maybe because Northern California's water was so cold, Gordy surmised.

But "The Duke" wanted everyone to see how fun and easy it could be. Only a handful of guys knew anything about surfing in Santa Cruz—let alone the rest of the world.

Besides the water temperature, Santa Cruz presented the perfect spot to ride waves, with its miles and miles of beaches that the waves broke upon.

"Everyone will be surfing by the time I leave this place," Duke said to a couple of the early surfers he met.

"But it is a little chilly."

He was right: People liked him, and they wanted more. Soon signs popped up, welcoming Duke. Reporters took photos and people came to see "the man visiting all of the way from Hawaii." Most people had never even heard of the islands.

Duke was tall, dark, and handsome. His teeth were large, shiny, and white as snow. And his personality won everyone over. He swam like a fish and rode the waves as though he spent more time in the water than he did on land. Some wondered whether maybe he had gills instead of lungs.

One day, Duke rode the Giant Dipper roller coaster on the boardwalk. Up and up the roller coaster clanked, and down it came, as fast as any wave he ever rode. Never before had he been on anything like it. It reminded him of the big waves he rode back home—only he was flying this time. He stretched his arms as far as they could go above his head, feeling the tickle in his stomach.

Later, he went into the water at Cowell's Beach and began doing handstands on his surfboard. He saw a pretty girl watching him and got out of the water.

"Do you surf?" he asked.

"Me?"

"Of course, *you!*"

"Why no, I could never get in the water."

Duke didn't wait for her to finish the sentence.

"Sure you could!"

She was in a bit of a panic.

"But I never did it before, and I, I..."

"How do you know anything about it until you try it?" he asked, offering his hand to her. He was just too hard to resist.

"All right! I will!"

As she ran into the water with him, you could hear her laughing, saying, "My mother is going to drop dead when she sees me!"

Just then, her mother came to the beach with lunch. She was all bundled up in a black wool bathing suit that covered her body from her neck to her knees. It weighed twenty pounds soaking wet, and on top of that, she wore black stockings and an oversized hat.

She carried a tray of food, filled with hamburgers, drinks, and dessert. She stood there for a moment, looked around, and couldn't find her daughter.

"Have you seen my daughter?" she asked around.

"She's out there," someone said, pointing to the ocean. Her daughter was riding with Duke on his surfboard.

"Hi, Mother!" she shouted, waving.

"Oh! For heaven's sakes!" her mother exclaimed as she dropped the tray of food.

By 1936, camaraderie had developed between the surfers who came to visit and the locals. Darren Steward invited them to store their surfboards in the basement of his family home. That's when the idea of forming the Santa Cruz Surfing Club came about. When the Stewards moved to a house on Bay Street with a barn behind it, the visitors were invited to use the loft of the barn not just for storing their boards, but also for sleeping. Since the barn was only three blocks from Cowell's Beach, it became a regular meeting place for all surfers, placing Santa Cruz on the map as one of the all-time best surf spots in the world.

"What a wonderful life," Gordy thought. "What a strange and wonderful life it has been."

FIFTY-FOUR

It was the last day of the semester before winter break. Rowanna leaned up against her desk, lecturing in her usual manner.

"How do you tell an entire civilization that you are sorry for the wrongful and massive slaying of its people?"

The history of Santa Cruz had come to an end in room number nine. The class had gotten together and bought a gift for Ms. Rowanna—a dozen red roses and a letter they had all contributed to. Giliano handed the flowers to Rowanna, and then Bliss and Jade got up and read the letter to their teacher.

Tearfully, Bliss read first.

"How can one express the remorse, sadness, and regret after generations of intentional torture, thievery, and destruction to each other? How could we ever repay a debt so deep?"

Then Bliss handed the paper over to Jade to read.

"May the curse be broken, and may we someday have mercy on ourselves. May we finally see what it really means to forgive and walk the talk of true restitution and unselfish justice. May we see the truth about forgiveness, but more importantly, may we someday really live it."

Jade handed the paper to Eric.

"May we learn from our mistakes and from the mistakes of our ancestors."

He passed the letter to Randy.

"May we carry our brothers in times of need and always re-member that our only true job in life is to be of service and to love ourselves and one another."

Randy looked over to Howard and smiled. He handed the letter over to Holly.

"May we never forget the simple things in life that really matter, like the moments that carry absolutely nothing else except one moment to the next."

Holly looked to the very back of the room and walked over to Tim, who was wearing his fitted black Humane Society T-shirt with a kitten on it. She handed him the paper, nudging him to read the last sentence.

"May we live in perfect harmony and finally realize that love is all we truly want."

He walked up to the front of the room and handed Rowanna the letter. Rowanna wiped her wet eyes, stood up from her desk, and straightened out her skirt.

"Very well, then. Looks like we did well." She nodded her head lovingly. "We all did very, very well indeed."

FIFTY-FIVE

Rowanna sat stout on a firm red couch at a television studio. People fussed around her with make-up brushes to soak up any last facial oil or blotches.

The talk show host, a platinum blonde in her forties, with a keen grasp on issues, was concerned about Rowanna.

"Are you okay, honey? Do you need some water or anything?"

"Oh, no, I may seem a little nervous—it's been years since I have been in front of the camera—but it's all coming back. I am just fine."

And she was perfectly fine. The crew was ready to roll.

"Good Morning, America!" The talk show host announced.

"This morning we have Rowanna O'Connor, who has just released her hit novel, *The Curse of Santa Cruz*.

"Rowanna, how does it feel to go from a history teacher to being number one on the bestseller list?"

"Well, it was certainly a change in my everyday life style. I am used to the same old routine and rather like it that way."

The host chuckled.

"How did you come up with the idea to write this book and where did you get your information? Is there really a curse?"

"I am not here to sell anybody on anything. It's not my job to tell people how or what to believe. I simply wanted to give the Ohlone Indian Nation a chance to have their voice heard.

"When I was a journalist for over ten years, I heard some rumors about a curse. That's when I started to investigate. As fate would have it, I had my own encounter with a suspected serial killer who was never identified.

"He beat me and left me for dead.

"After years of memory loss, I went back to school and earned my teaching credentials. I discovered a passion for California history as I taught high school students.

"The last class I taught before I retired was the best class I ever had on the history of Santa Cruz. We all taught each other. I will be forever grateful to those young, courageous adults.

"At the end of my final semester, I had a very special meeting with an Ohlone Elder who came to me in a dream. In the dream, she handed me a letter. When I woke up, it was in my hand. She told me to read it to as many people as I could. May I?"

Intrigued, the host agreed.

Rowanna pulled a piece of paper out of her pocket and began to read.

"What if...The Great Spirit just is—perfect, unchangeable, limitless, and everlasting, that which is you and I; we just forgot. Let's say the world and the universe is a dualistic experience, projected by human minds and based on the false idea of separation. What if people are acting out a dream of hate that is merely a reflection of what could never be duplicated?

"Buried deep within our subconscious is the seed of self-hatred because of a false idea of separation between our fellow human beings. The ego protects this lie.

"We ask ourselves: If there is a Great Spirit, how could he, she, or it let so many horrible things happen? The answer is, he doesn't.

"There is a Great Spirit, but he didn't make this world, this universe. We did. We tried to copy what could never be copied. And it remains in our mind.

"At some point, we must ask: 'What if?'

"What if we are trying to find our way back to reality and the all-encompassing truth is our destiny? What if to wake up from this tireless sleep is our job? And what if there is no such thing as space and time, left or right, up or down, and good or bad?

"What if it is all in our minds and we are now finally remembering, but only after countless lifetimes and civilizations—here as we know them and elsewhere as well—built and fallen, so old and so long ago, they are not even acknowledged in our history books?

"What if we had a shift in perception and finally realized that after all of that, even our perception meant nothing and that we must turn everything over on our way home to Love?

"And that everything really is: All for one and one for all.

"What if?"

The host needed to cut for a commercial break. A little shaken, she held her hand to her heart.

"Amazing, Rowanna. Simply amazing."

She showed the audience the cover of the black shiny book, depicting a white feather that dripped blood.

"Buy the book. *The Curse of Santa Cruz.* You won't be able to put it down. And now, we have to go to break."

The cameras were off. The host was shocked.

"Did a ghost really give you that letter?"

A group of ghostly Indians appeared behind the worried host. It was the Shaman, his wife, Tall-Boy, Woman-Girl, and the twins. There was a glowing light around them as they smiled at Rowanna when she replied calmly.

"Oh, come on now; you don't believe in ghosts, do you?"

ABOUT THE AUTHOR

Stephanie Michel attended the Lee Strasberg Institute and appeared in her first film as an actress at age seventeen. She then did general studies and script writing at Santa Monica College while appearing in various films, TV shows, commercials, and rock videos. She also worked with Robert Evans, *Playboy*, and Jay Bernstein, mega talent manager and film producer at CBS studios. She is a firm believer that positive thinking and a rich sense of humor is imperative for good mental health in the world as we know it today. She was a regular stand-up & (lay-down) comic at The Ice House, The Laugh Factory, The Comedy Store, and The Improv. She has completed several screenplays, TV pilots, and countless monologues.

Stephanie now resides in Hawaii with her daughter Pearl and her four dogs. She loves to write, work out, and go to the beach.

The Curse of Santa Cruz is her first novel.

$16.95

Made in the USA
San Bernardino, CA
09 August 2017